A
CHRISTMAS
HOME

ALSO BY GREG KINCAID

A Dog Named Christmas

Christmas with Tucker

A
CHRISTMAS
HOME

GREG KINCAID

CROWN PUBLISHERS

New York

Copyright © 2012 by Greg Kincaid

All rights reserved.
Published in the United States by Crown Publishers,
an imprint of the Crown Publishing Group,
a division of Random House, Inc., New York.

CROWN and the Crown colophon
are registered trademarks of Random House, Inc.

ISBN 978-0-307-95197-7

PRINTED IN THE UNITED STATES OF AMERICA

Jacket design: Megan McLaughlin
Jacket photographs: Debra Bardowicks/Oxford Scientific/Getty Images
(dog); Michael Mahovlich/Masterfile *(background)*

This book is

lovingly dedicated to

my youngest son,

Thomas Kincaid

(1990–2011)

A
CHRISTMAS
HOME

Prologue

* * * * * * * *

Early November

For several hours men in sweat-soaked uniforms walked in and out of the small bungalow. Each time they opened the front door, a chilly wind lifted the edges of the brown paper that had been put down to protect the floors. Dominated more by dandelions than bluegrass, the lawn on the side of the house facing the street had not been mowed in months. The FOR SALE sign cast a shadow on broken and discarded toys that lay in empty flower beds.

When the strangers first arrived, all their activity made the retriever edgy. She snapped her head up to better take in their scents and barked deeply. A woman, not yet thirty-five, but already wrinkled with disappointment, held the dog at bay. The dog would not yield. The barking made the woman nervous, so after a few minutes she put the retriever in the fenced-in backyard and went back to watching the strangers carrying boxes and furniture from the house, loading them into a long white beached whale of a truck parked along the curb.

The men maneuvered a few larger pieces of furniture out the back door and through the dog's yard. They attempted to befriend the retriever with soft, beckoning voices, but sensing the woman's suspicions and fears, the dog stood steadfast and only answered with muted growls through clenched teeth.

The dog was a three-year-old female of steady temperament (under normal conditions) and intelligence, originating from the stoic golden retriever bloodlines of her mother. Her spectacular thick and soft, creamy coat hued with soft white fur, and her loyal and fearless heart came straight from her father: a Great Pyrenees.

In addition to the dog and the woman, two children lived in the bungalow. It was the only home the boy and girl had ever known. Their mother's vague explanation for the move—that the bank now owned the house—was beyond their comprehension, and they were confused. At about the same time the movers were completing their work, the school bus let the children off at the corner. As they approached their house, they found it very unsettling to see everything they owned loaded inside a truck.

It seemed strange to return to their home emptied of all their belongings. A variety of hidden debris was all there was left— dust, dog hair, pennies, Cheetos, crayons, matchbooks, and little scraps of paper with faded phone numbers, all small memories of times past. The children walked through the house like refugees, stunned by the ghostly quiet. The youngest child, a six-year-old boy with thick, dark hair, draped his small arms around the retriever they called Gracie. There were so many things the boy could not understand. At the top of the list was why they had to leave their home and this dog he loved so much. He had cried and cried and still no one could answer what seemed to him such a simple question. Why? Even his teachers put their arms around him and awkwardly strung together words that were too abstract for him to comprehend, like "sometimes life takes hard turns."

The boy's older sister, a tall and gangly nine-year-old, was carrying a small gym bag that her mother was allowing her to take with her in the car. She pulled out a note she had written while the other children played at recess earlier in the day. The paper had a hole punched in the corner with a piece of red ribbon threaded through for tying the note to the dog's collar. The outside of the note bore the name Gracie.

The children's mother deposited two large plastic buckets in the yard. She sighed and wished that the bank would accept her children's tears in lieu of ten months of delinquent mortgage payments. The red bucket was filled to the brim with four gallons of water, and the green bucket held the bargain-brand dog food they could barely afford. When she got out of town, she would call the local shelter and anonymously report the dog as abandoned. She knew she should take the dog there herself, but she couldn't stand the thought of one more humiliating encounter.

The woman unwound her children's arms from around the dog. She took them by the hands and directed them out of the backyard, where only a few days earlier they'd played so *happily and life seemed predictable and full of promise. Things had gone wrong for the woman and her family very quickly; first, the divorce; then her ex lost his job and could no longer pay child support; and then she'd lost her own job when her employer pulled up stakes from Crossing Trails. The foreclosure was inevitable. When her son began to sob inconsolably, she held him close to her, not saying a word. There were no words, she thought. No words.*

The woman shut the backyard gate behind her and did not allow herself to look back as she headed for the packed car in the driveway. She wanted to stay strong for her children. Life might knock her down, but she would get up and keep walking, one step at a time. She deeply regretted leaving Gracie behind— she loved the dog as much as the children did—but it was a sacrifice she knew she had to make. She swallowed hard and hoped that the shelter would find a good home for the dog.

Gracie pressed her face against the gate, barked, and then began circling nervously around the yard. She could see the driveway from the gate and watched the familiar car pull out, the boy and girl waving back at her. Then they were gone. But what did it matter? They always returned.

As dusk turned to night, no one came back. The dog was anxious and confused. The next morning, no one took her for a walk, poured fresh water or food into the plastic buckets, or let her in the house. The day progressed but still there was no television, no children's voices. No one threw her a ball or sat beside her as the sun set in the sky, talking about homework or playground bullies.

The next day, the dog accidentally knocked over what little water was left in her bucket. She panted, and as the hours passed her throat and mouth became dry and chalky. She could smell and sense water beyond the fence that confined her. Tantalizingly near, water sprayed from the sprinklers in the neighbor's yard; she could hear it swirling in washing machines and dishwashers and from a neighbor's hose where a boy was washing his father's car. Gracie needed to get out, needed to get beyond the fence, needed to feel wetness on her tongue. She pawed at the gate and barked until she could bark no more. Her house was on a corner, and the neighbors next door were elderly and did not hear well. No one came.

The white retriever spent the day whimpering and drifting in and out of a deep sleep.

Late in the afternoon the back gate opened and a man with a camera began taking pictures and measurements of the yard. Gracie slowly opened her eyes and watched the man as if she were in a dream. The man coughed and the dog jumped, now alert. With all the energy she could muster, she hunched low into a submissive position and walked toward the stranger. The man was startled but quickly put his camera on the ground and brushed the dog's head with his hand.

"Another one abandoned," he muttered to himself. While petting her, he found the paper tied to the dog's collar. Carefully he undid the red ribbon knot, unfolded the note, and read it.

Our dog's name is Gracie. She is the very best dog in the world. We love her, but we have to leave her because we don't have a house anymore. Please take good care of her and she'll take good care of you.

Signed, Meagan

The man stared at the note and then looked into the dog's eyes. "Sorry, Gracie," he said. "The world is upside down right now."

The man took the dog's bucket and walked over to a spigot on the side of the house. He turned it and nothing happened. They shut the water off, *he thought. Looking around he saw a hose on the other side of the fence. He left the dog, opened the gate, and quickly stole across the neighbor's driveway, turned on the spigot, and filled the dog's bucket. He sighed. "So close and yet so far away," he murmured.*

The man walked back and put the bucket in front of the dog. Without hesitation, Gracie's tongue touched the clear liquid and at first it stung, but then the feeling of pain turned to joy and the dog lapped for a very long time. "This is happening a lot, old girl," the man said. "Houses being foreclosed, families forced out, beautiful animals like you being left behind. I kind of hate my job sometimes."

The local animal shelter where he brought these abandoned pets called them foreclosure dogs and gave them a host of names that reflected their owner's plight, like Past Due, ARM, and Subprime. Many of the owners reasoned that the bank, a neighbor, the police—surely someone—would come and care for their pet. "Let me just take some pictures, girl, and I'll help you out, okay?" He watched her drink deeply and ran his fingers through her long white coat. The dog looked sad but smelled clean. "You're a beautiful dog, aren't you? If I wasn't struggling myself, I'd take you home with me right now."

When she finished drinking, Gracie nuzzled the man's wrist appreciatively. The man stood and fumbled in his pocket for the keys to the house. He pulled them out, unlocked the back door, and entered to take measurements and pictures and complete his report so the bank could market the foreclosed property. In thirty minutes he was finished and returned to check on the dog. She was not where he had left her. He searched about the yard, but she was nowhere to be seen.

"Oh, shoot," he said, catching sight of the wide-open gate that he'd forgotten to latch. Perhaps the dog had just now escaped, and he moved quickly to the front yard hoping to find her there. He looked down the narrow street lined with modest homes, many also for sale, and spotted her at the far end of the block. He yelled to get her attention and began to follow her. "Here girl. Come on back!" He put his fingers to his mouth and let out a loud whistle.

The dog was meandering down the middle of the road but ignored his pleas to return.

"Come on back!" he shouted again, but it was too late.

A car came around the corner and its horn issued a shrill warning. Startled, the dog reflexively bolted straight into the path of the car. Tires screeched. Impact. The retriever was tossed to the side of the road. Stunned and frightened, she struggled to get up, but it was not possible. She breathed deeply and her heart raced out of fear. Confused and hurt, she tried to crawl further off the road to safety.

As the man from the bank trotted toward Gracie, car doors slammed and two people emerged from the car before he could reach her. The young female driver immediately began to wail, "Oh, Mom, I hit her! I didn't even see her!"

"Laura," her mother said, reaching out and wrapping her hand around the thin arm of her fair-haired daughter. "It wasn't your fault. The dog ran out in front of you."

Still frightened but trying to regain her composure, the girl clutched her mother's elbow. "We have to . . . try . . . to help." She stepped slowly closer, holding her mother's arm for support, and desperately hoping that the retriever was not dead. The dog lifted her head but didn't move.

Stunned, like any injured animal, the dog sensed her own vulnerability. She growled, warning the two women to keep their distance.

"What should we do?" the mother asked.

Laura reached down and tried to comfort the dog, but Gracie growled again, so she backed away. She thought a moment and got the words straight in her head before speaking. "I'll call Todd." She pulled her cell phone from her pocket and hit his number on her speed dial.

CHAPTER I

. . . .

One Year Later

PEOPLE WOULD look at the old black Lab and say, "Christmas. That's an unusual name for a dog." In the beginning, George would explain how the Lab was supposed to have been a temporary holiday guest, a brief fostering project to help out the local animal shelter. His youngest son, Todd, thought the name Christmas was a good fit. Now, nearly four years later, the dog had found a permanent home with the McCray family, and George was inclined to lean down, hug his canine friend around the neck, and say, "Best Christmas present I ever got!"

Christmas was resting his head on Todd's lap in the backseat of the car as they drove down Main Street that evening. George's wife, Mary Ann, and Todd chatted back and forth about the weather—lightly falling snow, smoky gray skies, and a low howling northwest wind. George, a pragmatic sort, smiled at the notion, but wondered if they shouldn't have named the lab Elmer, like the glue. The dog bound and knitted his family together.

The elder McCray tried to park in the small municipal lot that flanked the west side of Crossing Trails Town Hall, but it was already jammed with cars. The turnout for that night's town hall meeting was going to be huge, particularly for a town of less than two thousand residents. So much was hanging in the balance.

George turned back onto Main Street and drove north for two more blocks before finding a space in front of what had been the barbershop but was now a Dollar General Store—a sign of the times. Though many older businesses like the hardware store and the diner had managed to hang on, the growing number of discount stores suggested that the town's better days were visible only in the rearview mirror. Once within this tiny six-block area they still called "downtown" there had been a bakery, a movie theater, clothing stores, a Ford dealership, a furniture shop, and much more. Still, the Crossing Trails Chamber of Commerce boasted thirty-four members. The town just *had* to survive, George thought. *Right?* Any other answer seemed inconceivable.

Many of the original stately brick buildings had survived, but there were also plenty of newer, cheaper-looking steel-and-concrete structures, quite a few sporting FOR RENT OR SALE signs. George was continually amazed at the way the town had changed, particularly in the last several years as the exodus of young people from the rural farming community continued. At least his children, all living within driving distance, had not strayed too far from the McCray homestead. Todd was closest of all.

"Looks like a good turnout for the meeting," George observed.

"As it should be. People are worried." Mary Ann buttoned up her coat and collected her purse from the floor of the car. She turned around and poked at her son's knee. "Let's go."

Todd undid his seat belt and started to get out of the backseat with his headphones still attached and his iPod playing a Scotty McCreery tune that he did his best to adopt as his own. Once completely out of the car, he broke out with the chorus, "I love you *this* big!" As Todd stretched out his arms, Mary Ann stepped into his embrace, and they repeated the lyrics together. Mary Ann smiled at life. Being a music teacher and having a tone-deaf son was beyond ironic.

George opened the other rear passenger door. When Christmas jumped out, he snapped a leash on the dog's collar and gave him a gentle pat on the head. "Good boy. You've got work to do tonight, don't you?"

There was an unusual urgency to that night's town hall meeting. Earlier in the week *The Prairie Star*—Crossing

Trail's newspaper, once daily, but now weekly—had reported that the mayor would discuss the town's latest economic setback. After fifty years, Midwest Trailer and Hitch had officially called it quits. Horse ownership was at an all-time low, as were trailer sales, and the town's largest employer was going out of business.

The survival of Crossing Trails was being threatened by a combination of factors that could be overcome only by an intense collaborative effort. Severe cost-cutting measures were inevitable, and everyone knew it. The lead story in *The Prairie Star* indicated that services that had once been taken for granted were now at risk. Like a virus at a day care, the rumors spread up and down Main Street in the close-knit town. People had moved right past worried and were dashing toward panicked.

The McCrays and other families had watched as smaller rural communities in the surrounding counties had eliminated or consolidated fire and police departments, closed schools and libraries, shut hospitals, and all but died. They couldn't help wondering if the same spiral had been set in motion in their town.

George, Todd, and Mary Ann walked south down Main Street as a light fog settled in. Christmas loitered, sniffing at the occasional fire hydrant. The outside temperature on this early December evening was warmer than the snow-covered ground. The slushy sidewalk was dangerously slick and uneven in places, so they walked carefully, with Todd in the middle, holding on to his parents' hands with a firm, youthful grip that kept them from slipping.

Mary Ann liked it that her adult son would still hold his parents' hands. For some it might be considered a sign of his disability, but for her it meant so much more. When he was little, he held her hand for physical support; when he was older, he did it for emotional reassurance. It was his way of checking to make sure that his mother was there for him as he navigated through a world that did not always make sense to him. Later still, holding his parents' hands became a simple and honest way to show his unabashed love. While his grip still sent some of these ancient family messages, it was not lost on her that there was something new going on. Todd was using his strength to hold *them* up. She wondered if George was having anywhere near the same thought, or if Todd had an inkling of how the roles of parent and child were constantly being renegotiated with the passage of time.

In the storefront windows many of the merchants had made some effort to showcase their Christmas goods. Green holly and blinking white lights hung from the wood poles and brass rings that previous generations had used to tie off their horses. Falling under the dim light, cast by the old-fashioned streetlights, were little bits of intermittent snow blowing through the dark night sky.

With his jet-black coat, Christmas was hard to see as he tagged along, content, with his family.

The dog was a local legend in Crossing Trails. It was hard to know where the truth about Christmas ended and the exaggeration began; both George and Todd were inclined to embellish his exploits. Whether Christmas had really taken on a mountain lion and won, understood more than fifty words, or could read your thoughts didn't matter to most people. What they loved most about the dog was the joy he brought to the McCray family and every other human he met. That was magic enough.

Both Todd and George described Christmas as "my dog." However convenient, this was not entirely accurate. Like blue skies, small children, and the air we breathe, dogs can be shared, loved, and enjoyed but not owned. Partnership, yes. Ownership, no. That's the way it has always been between dogs and humans.

The foursome entered the crowded meeting room of City Hall. Todd's boss at the shelter, Hayley Donaldson, had promised to save them seats near the back, where Christmas could rest out of the way before he went to work. The McCrays looked around but could not find Hayley, so they claimed four chairs at the back of the room and sat down.

Todd took the aisle seat and gave the command for Christmas to sit, out of the flow of traffic. He pulled an index card from his pocket with a list on it. Hayley loved lists. She was always giving him lists. Todd smiled to himself as he thought about the lists. He would often tease Hayley by greeting her with his hand extended. When she looked at him quizzically, he would say, "Waiting for my list!"

Earlier that day she had written on an index card the things she wanted him and Christmas to do at the town hall meeting. At times it irritated Todd that she made so many lists telling him to do things he didn't need her to tell him to do. When he complained about it to her, she just said, "I make lists for me, so what's wrong with making them for you?"

Todd stuffed the index card back in his pocket, and as he did a funny thought caused him to laugh out loud. Tomorrow he would make a list and give it to Hayley. It would say, "Quit making lists!"

George looked up at his son wondering why he was chuckling. "What's so amusing?"

Sometimes other people did not find the same things funny that Todd did, so he had slowly grown guarded about sharing his sense of humor—even with his mom and dad. He was afraid that it did not make him look smart. "I was just thinking about something at work."

George smiled reassuringly, picking up on Todd's reluctance to explain himself further. In fact, as someone who loved to laugh when he could, George very much enjoyed Todd's sense of humor and didn't care whether or not his son looked smart.

George returned his attention to the room. No one had bothered to plug the Christmas tree lights in on the mayor's Christmas tree. Fake gift boxes had been haphazardly spread about the base. All the faux gifts were wrapped in the same green paper, and most were ripped in several places. Many of the bows and ribbons had slipped off. George took one look at the pathetic tree, went over to the wall socket, and plugged in the lights. It looked only marginally better. He shrugged and returned to his seat between Todd and Mary Ann.

The McCrays spotted many familiar faces as more people began to stream into the increasingly crowded room; it seemed that most of the families they knew in Cherokee County were represented here tonight. This meeting had definitely captured everyone's attention. While George said his hellos to friends and neighbors, Mary Ann turned around and glanced at the entrance to watch the people coming in. Then she caught sight of a scene unfolding in the small glass-walled conference room across from the main meeting hall. She nudged George. "Look out there," she said softly.

Though they could not hear the conversation, it was obvious to the two of them that Hayley Donaldson was having a heated discussion with the mayor and the city manager. She was throwing her hands up in the air as if to say *What gives?* She was a tall, self-assured, and confident woman—fit and strong from handling dogs. "That looks bad," George said quietly, while thinking to himself that he wouldn't want to be on the receiving end in a heated exchange with that young lady.

Todd, oblivious to the scene, pulled Christmas close

to him and checked his pockets to make sure he had remembered the training treats. That was number four on Hayley's list. He grinned again.

The door to the conference room flew open and Hayley stepped out into the hall that separated the smaller room from the main hall. She saw the McCray family in the last row and moved quickly toward them, greeting Todd and Christmas briefly before taking the seat next to Mary Ann, who sensed her distress the moment she saw her. "I'm so darn mad, I can't talk," she whispered to Mary Ann. She continued to glare out into space, and soon angry tears began to stream down her cheeks.

Mary Ann took her by the arm. "Hayley, what's wrong?"

In high school Hayley had been one of Mary Ann's favorite students, in every way a responsible and dedicated young woman. She had been one of the stars on the debate team and had never lost her composure easily. Mary Ann tended to remain protective of her former students. She tried again, "What happened? Tell me."

"You're not going to believe this. I can't believe it."

"What?" Mary Ann pleaded.

Hayley nodded her head in Todd's direction and then leaned over to whisper in her favorite teacher's ear, "They want to close the shelter. Like, now."

"No!" Mary Ann gasped. She could not help her own reaction but didn't want Todd to overhear. "Come with me," she said, standing. Todd and George looked up as the two women stepped into the aisle. Mary Ann clutched Hayley's elbow and said, "Just a quick trip to the ladies' room before this meeting starts." George looked at Mary Ann and nodded, knowing full well that something else was going on.

Once in the hallway, struggling to keep her voice even, Mary Ann continued, "Why in the world would they do that?"

Hayley spoke softly and tried to sum up her conversation with the mayor. "As usual: it's all about money. The county is no longer willing to fund its half of the shelter's expenses. The town has its own money problems. Mayor McDaniel told me that they want us to close. We're done."

Mary Ann's voice rose uncontrollably. "That's impossible. Where will the dogs go?"

Several people milling in the hallway began to notice their conversation. Hayley led Mary Ann a few steps farther away from the meeting room and continued her explanation. "Mayor McDaniel may know something about real estate, but she doesn't know squat about animal shelters. She must think that we can put fifty-plus dogs and cats on the corner and someone will just pick them up. I had to scream at her just so she would agree to let us stay open till the end of the year."

"Why is the county backing out?" Mary Ann asked.

"The shelter needs lots of repairs. The roof, the plumbing, the heating, and the air-conditioning are all old."

"So why can't they just fix it?"

"They needed the money for other things, so they sold our building. We have to vacate by December 31. They are going to demolish the shelter to make room for a convenience store! I'm just so mad I can't stand it!"

Mary Ann looked toward the meeting room. "Does Todd know?"

"No. I just found out myself."

"They gave you no warning?"

"A couple of months ago, and then again several weeks ago, the city manager told me that there were money problems and problems with our lease, too." Hayley again started to choke on her words. "They never told me this could happen. I thought they would work it out. I just didn't take the whole thing seriously." She calmed herself. "I should have seen it coming."

"But how could you have seen this coming?" Mary Ann asked.

"It's happening to lots of shelters. Dogs can't vote. That makes them an easy target for budget cuts. I didn't think it could happen to us. Not in Crossing Trails. I thought we were different."

"This is awful, Hayley. I'm so sorry." While Mary Ann meant every word she said, her thoughts began turning closer to home. "What's going to happen to those dogs?" she repeated. "Todd is going to be crushed."

Hayley could hear the mayor and the city manager calling the meeting to order. "We better go back in."

Mary Ann grabbed Hayley's arm. "Wait. Are they going to announce this tonight?"

Hayley tried to reassure her. "No. I asked them to wait

until I could tell Todd, Doc Pelot, and our volunteers. They're all going to be sick."

"So what do we do?" Mary Ann asked.

"The mayor wants Todd and me to go ahead with our presentation. I suppose it's more important than ever. Let's get through tonight and tomorrow, and then we'll try to figure this mess out."

Mary Ann shook her head, and the two of them returned to their seats. After introducing her colleague, Mayor Annie McDaniel opened the floor for community announcements. A representative from the local retirement center described their annual holiday open house and choir performance, *Over the Hill, but Not Under It!*

The high school principal, Mary Ann's boss, talked next about a number of athletic events, including a trip to the state championship for the football team and a strong start to basketball season, encouraging local fans to come out and support the town's young players at their upcoming games.

The mayor then turned to the more urgent business at hand. "I'm afraid the focus for tonight's meeting is a difficult subject. As I'm sure you all know by now, Midwest Trailer and Hitch shut its doors in September, and we are certainly feeling the fallout around here. Many of our merchants are reporting slower holiday sales, and plenty of you are looking for employment and not finding it. The number of homes listed for sale has quadrupled, and you've undoubtedly noticed the growing number of downtown storefronts with 'For Rent' signs posted. The town's tax revenues are shrinking. My message tonight is that now, more than ever, we must pull together and not panic. To survive we have to make difficult choices and cut expenses. We are here to solicit ideas on how Crossing Trails might best respond to the closing of Midwest Trailer and Hitch. We also need to discuss spending cuts and how we can lessen their impact on our community. So let's get started."

A slight murmur ran through the audience. A man in overalls with a gray-and-white beard raised his hand and asked if there was any chance that the trailer company might reopen. The mayor supplied the easy answer. "No."

Annie McDaniel's mayoral position was unpaid, but she took it seriously. She saw this town hall meeting as an opportunity for using her leadership to rally the townspeople. She knew that things could go a couple of different ways. Her main worry was that a lot of scared people would expect her, or more generally the town, to fix problems that were in many ways outside the town's scope of power. She wanted the meeting to go in a different direction. She wanted to give people the sense of hope that comes from doing and not demanding.

The mayor exhaled and decided to jump in with what she considered a well-calculated gamble. After picking up a folder from the podium and ignoring a number of raised hands, she cleared her throat and continued. "I'm here tonight to ask you to help one another. I have made a list of services that the city will no longer be able to afford. This doesn't mean these services aren't important, or that we don't care; it just means that we can no longer afford to offer them. I'm going to keep this list"—she held the list high in the air before continuing—"at City Hall. I hope each of you will come by and look it over."

Mayor McDaniel tried to gauge her audience's reaction. Seeing only a few scowls, she continued. "Let me give you an example. Starting January first, we will no longer be able to offer the transportation van for the elderly. Believe it or not, that alone is costing us over fifty thousand dollars a year. We need volunteers to take over this responsibility. The Wellness Center will keep a list of folks needing rides. If you have some elderly friends, neighbors, or relatives, I hope you'll help them out."

She looked at the shocked faces in the room and heard the grumbling commence. She knew it was going to get worse. She took a long breath and continued, "We have to cut the city payroll by twenty percent. To do this we have decided to institute an immediate hiring freeze. We are also planning to cut back the library's operating hours and suspend most parks-and-recreation services, including the municipal pool and tennis courts. There are more programs that must be trimmed. We will be making these decisions shortly. It's either make these cuts or go bankrupt; we have no choice."

The mayor then located Hayley in the audience and

continued, "The animal shelter desperately needs our help and soon," she said. Just by mentioning the shelter in the same breath as the other cuts, she knew that many residents would suspect that the shelter was on the chopping block. "Hayley Donaldson, I wonder if you would tell us about the shelter's annual holiday adoption program, which is going to be even more urgent this year than ever."

Hayley tried her best to keep her composure as she made her way to the front of the room. She stood next to the mayor and spoke into the microphone. "This year we have fifty-six cats and dogs that need families just like yours to put a roof over their heads. As the mayor said, this is an area where the community needs to accept and share responsibility. If you have the space for a dog or cat in your life, I hope you'll come by and see us. Every year I'm amazed at the quality of our shelter guests. A common misconception is that our dogs and cats have been rejected by families and left at the shelter for a good reason. That's rarely the case. Within two weeks after the trailer company closed their doors, we took in over thirty dogs and cats. Almost without exception these are great pets. I want to show you a fantastic rescue dog."

On cue Todd McCray stood up. The audience traced Hayley's line of sight back to Todd and shifted their attention to him. "A few years back, we had a very special guest living with us, and I thought you might like to meet him. Some of you already know this character, since he is pretty good at making friends." She motioned with her hand.

"Todd, why don't you bring Christmas up here and show him off?"

Todd stood up and trotted briskly to the front of the room with a leash in one hand and a folding chair in the other. Christmas seemed to enjoy being the center of attention. He followed Todd to the front of the meeting room. Hands reached out to pat him lovingly as he passed by. No one was a stranger to this dog.

When Todd and Christmas were positioned beside her, Hayley asked, "Todd, is it possible to get a good dog at an animal shelter?"

Todd spoke the words that Hayley had carefully scripted on his index card. "Yes, it is. Some of the very best dogs in the world live at our shelter."

"Your family adopted this dog from us. Would you show us what he can do?"

Todd unfolded the chair with the back facing the audience. He patted the seat and commanded, "Up!"

Christmas jumped into the chair and rested his front paws on the seatback, then looked back at Todd for his next direction.

Todd commanded, "Wave." The dog lifted his front paw and set it back down on the chair several times in what looked surprisingly like a friendly greeting to the audience. Todd reached in his coat pocket and gave Christmas a training reward. He commanded, "Say 'hello.'" Christmas let out a nice loud bark and got hearty applause for it.

Hayley put her hand on Todd's shoulder. "Thanks, Todd.

I hope all of you will come out to the shelter and consider adopting a dog or cat for Christmas this year. We've got some great ones and they *really* need homes!"

The mayor took the floor again and thanked Hayley, who returned to sit with the McCrays. The mayor sighed and then continued down her list of cuts, layoffs, and eliminations.

As the evening continued, an unsettling feeling began to grip George, Mary Ann, Hayley, and many of the others in the room. Could the community adapt? Would Crossing Trails survive? Or would their town just dry up and blow away like so many other small rural communities? What had seemed unthinkable months and years ago now seemed possible. The prospect made George feel a little sick to his stomach.

Todd walked back down the aisle and stopped in front of his dad's chair. He bent over and whispered in his ear, "I'm going to the Wellness Center. Laura wants me to help her with something. Will you pick me up when you're done?"

George nodded. "We'll see you in an hour or so." Todd handed the leash to George. Christmas scooted over a few inches, and George sank his fingers into his thick fur. George didn't know if he was prouder of his old black Lab or his son. His work completed, Christmas yawned and stretched out comfortably on the floor of the meeting hall.

THE CROSSING Trails Wellness Center integrated many medical services into one building. Separately, the community could not sustain a hospital, a nursing home, a health clinic, and a rehab facility, so they combined these functions all under one roof. Although duly certified, it had by necessity evolved along unorthodox lines, and the hiring of Laura Jordan was a case in point. At most hospitals, trying to hire a young LPN who worked with a service dog would trigger a managerial and legal cyclone that would cause the HR person to dive for cover. At the Crossing Trails Wellness Center, the challenge had been addressed with remarkably little hand-wringing. "Why not give it a try?"

Laura was twenty-four years old, slender, and not very tall, with long blond hair, soft brown eyes, and a welcoming smile. Because she was always quick with a helping hand and a kind word, most of her colleagues and patients did not immediately notice when she moved slowly on some days. Her rheumatoid arthritis would come and go like an unwelcome houseguest. When it arrived, she walked stiffly and sometimes needed assistance sitting down and getting up again.

Under her photo this month—and not for the first time—was a small sign that read EMPLOYEE OF THE MONTH: LAURA JORDAN AND HER SERVICE DOG, GRACIE.

More than one patient who checked in at the reception area of the Wellness Center looked at the photo and asked, "Can she be my nurse?"

The receptionist would grin and say, "You'll have to get in line—she has a long waiting list!"

It turned out that Gracie was capable of doing a lot more than helping Laura up and down from a chair and fetching dropped objects. Gracie had an entire set of skills that had been slowly noted and assessed at the Wellness Center. For medically trained professionals, these skills were sometimes hard to believe or understand. The dog was accomplishing tasks that weren't in the textbooks. At least, not yet.

Gracie would stand patiently by a bed with a patient's left hand drooped over the bedrail and resting on the dog's furry white head while Laura took blood pressure measurements and asked about the person's pain levels and symptoms. Something remarkable happened. It was right in the medical records and not subject to cynical guffawing. When measured and charted over several shifts, for a statistically significant number of patients, pain levels, heart rates, and blood pressure consistently dropped in the soothing presence of the dog. Gracie was a healer of a different variety.

The dog intuitively offered something that many sick people needed. Laura would sit in a chair beside the bed and talk with a patient for a few minutes, waiting to see if Gracie felt the invitation to interact. If Gracie did, Laura would pull gently on the service dog harness that kept Gracie close to her. When given permission, Gracie would put her front legs up on the bed so the patient could cradle her furry white face in their hands and feel the dog's warmth. Within sixty seconds, a healing exchange occurred. Depressed faces lit. Anxiety-ridden minds relaxed. Patients expressed feelings of gratitude. They felt safe and cared for in a unique way that was not typically experienced in a hospital setting.

Todd jogged the two blocks from the town hall to the Wellness Center. He met Laura in the lobby. While she hung up his coat, Todd told her all about his dog's fine performance that evening at the town hall meeting. Todd patted Gracie affectionately, looked up at Laura, and gave his little *what's up?* shrug that was always delivered with a friendly twinkle from his sky-blue eyes. "What do you want me to help you with?"

Laura led Todd to the closed door of a supply closet just past the reception area. Inside were stacks of boxes. For those patients who would be staying at the Wellness Center over the holiday, their family members were invited to leave one average-sized box with the patient's name and room number written on the outside. They were to enclose in the box those familiar holiday objects that would help make their loved one feel at home for Christmas.

Almost without exception, the one-box rule was broken. Also stuffed in the closet—with apologetic little notes—were assorted extras, including trees, stockings, ornaments, large framed photographs, nativity scenes, stuffed reindeers, flashing lights, angels, and miniature Santa Clauses.

Laura turned on the light and tapped at one of the boxes with her foot. "Todd, would you pull that one out for me?"

"What for?"

"You'll see."

She set their course. "This one is for Mrs. Walker. She's in Room 211."

Todd picked up the box and started to walk down the corridor for the nursing home wing of the Wellness Center. "What's wrong with her?" Todd asked Laura.

"She's very old and has dementia." There was no reason for Todd to be familiar with Mrs. Walker's condition, so

Laura explained, "That's when you forget lots of things and are confused most of the time."

Todd shrugged. "Maybe I have dementia?"

"Don't say that, Todd! You don't have dementia. You'll see when you meet her. We all forget sometimes. She forgets most of the time. Get the difference?"

"Got it," Todd said. "I think."

Laura laughed and watched a red stocking fall out of the box. "Gracie, help us out." She pointed to the stocking, released the dog, and commanded, "Fetch!" Gracie retrieved the red felt stocking, gently took it in her mouth, and returned to Laura's side.

Mrs. Walker was ninety-four and had lived in Crossing Trails her whole life. She very much liked her pink flannel robe and warm, fleece-lined slippers—so much so that she rarely wore anything else. Earlier that afternoon, when Laura told her she would be coming by later to help ready her room for Christmas, Mrs. Walker had decided to dress for the occasion. Mrs. Walker had a hard time remembering many of the essential details of her long life history—particularly the names and faces of her assorted grandchildren and great-grandchildren. She figured Laura must have been some part of her family. She also had a very hard time hearing, which is why she thought that Laura had said that today was Christmas.

Mrs. Walker had put on her best red-and-green Christmas dress, her white pearls that her husband had given her on their sixty-fifth wedding anniversary, and a blue cardigan sweater. She sat in her recliner and waited for the festivities to begin.

Laura knocked and stuck her head inside the door, "Mrs. Walker, may we come in?"

The still-proud woman struggled to stand up and steady herself over her walker. "Yes, please come in!" Once she was up, she moved the walker aside. "Merry Christmas!"

Not wanting to spend the next ten minutes setting things straight for her, Laura just motioned Todd to join her. Todd entered the room and set the box down on the floor. Laura and Gracie moved closer, and Laura raised her voice. "Mrs. Walker, this is my friend Todd. We're going to set up some Christmas decorations for you."

Mrs. Walker extended her right hand. Todd took it gently in his own.

"How nice of you to visit me on Christmas." She glanced down at the box that was resting beside her. "You didn't need to bring me anything."

She sat back down and sized up her pair of visitors and the dog that was tagging along. "What a lovely dog!" Her eyes became bright and excited. "Is she yours?"

Laura lightly put an arm around the old woman's frail

shoulders and tried to explain the purpose of their visit. "Yes, she's my dog. Now, why don't you rest and let Todd and me decorate your room for you?"

"That would be very nice."

Although Mrs. Walker did not remember her, Gracie knew Mrs. Walker quite well. She had visited her almost every day for the last six months. Gracie stood beside her, wagging her tail eagerly.

Mrs. Walker did remember the dog that she and her brothers had owned when they were growing up. It was a black-and-white collie mix. Even though she was not quite certain why this dog was in her room, she could not have received a nicer gift. As she petted the dog's head, she felt something. It reminded her of when she was a girl and had been playing outside in the cold for a very long time with her brothers and their dog Judy, coming back inside where it was warm and safe, and resting beside the fire that burned in the old potbellied stove so her frozen fingers and toes could thaw out and come back to life. With some effort, Mrs. Walker leaned over and put her arms around Gracie. She pulled the white dog closer so she could bury her face in the dog's furry neck. Gracie stood there patiently and made small whimpering noises.

"She's a fine dog. What's her name?"

Laura looked up from the box of treasures. "Gracie."

"Ahh," the old woman replied. "It's a good name for her." She closed her eyes and let the deep and warm feelings the dog generated resonate inside her heart like the vibrations inside a bass kettledrum.

Laura pointed to the box. "Gracie." When she was sure she had the dog's attention, she completed the command, "Fetch." Gracie walked over to the box, gently took one of the cardboard flaps in her mouth, and pulled the box over to Laura. "Good girl, Gracie." Gracie sat and waited for her next instruction. Laura then pointed to Mrs. Walker and said, "Patient." Gracie returned to Mrs. Walker's side and sat close to her so the old woman could run her hands through the dog's thick white coat.

Twenty minutes later Mrs. Walker was asleep in her chair, with her old wrinkled hand still resting on Gracie's head.

Laura reached in the box and pulled out a small nativity scene. "This will look great on the console." She arranged the pieces as best she could while Todd rummaged through the box for the next decoration to set out.

Todd dug deeper into the box and pulled out a star that had been fixed rather awkwardly onto a plastic base so that it could rest on a tabletop. At first glance it looked more like a hat than a Christmas decoration. Todd grinned. "I know where this belongs!" He walked over to Laura and unceremoniously crowned her.

Laura laughed. Todd steadied the star from tumbling to the ground with his hands lingering for a few seconds on the top of her head. "Now you look like a Christmas angel, Laura," he said, his blue eyes dancing.

Laura smiled and suddenly blushed. "As a Christmas angel, I order you to put the star back on the table and get to work!"

❄

"Where are you staying tonight?" Todd asked the dog just before shutting the car door. When Christmas didn't budge, Todd shrugged, waved good-bye, and headed in the direction of his cabin, a small structure that rested at the bottom of the hill, well within view of his parent's watchful eyes. With the town hall meeting behind them, and their son collected from the Wellness Center and restored to his own home, Mary Ann and George returned to the old farmhouse on the top of the hill and nestled on the sofa with Christmas to watch the rest of the late night news.

Mary Ann reconfigured a question she had already asked George several times. "So you think he'll take the shelter closing in stride?"

Each time she asked, George parceled out a few more thoughts. "I don't know for sure. I think it'll take time, maybe even a few days, for him to figure out what this really means. With the economy the way it is, he'll be competing with lots of folks for employment. We're not charging him rent to stay in the old cabin. His truck is paid for. He doesn't need to make much money to get by."

Mary Ann stiffened. "George, is 'getting by' the goal

you have for him? You know, he's never had an interview or filled out a job application. It won't be easy for him. He may need help. This shelter has been such a blessing. I can't imagine him working anywhere else. Frankly, I'm not sure he can."

"You're right that it won't be easy, but he's not a child anymore, and there are plenty of ways he can earn a living—even if it takes time for him to find his way."

Mary Ann placed her latest knitting project in a large straw basket beside the sofa. George knew that this was the signal that his wife was about to get down to the meat of the issue. "I'm afraid that Todd may drown without that shelter job. We should be prepared to throw him a lifeline."

"What do you mean?" George asked.

"Todd is sensitive. I'm afraid he'll unravel if he's left to flip hamburgers the rest of his life. We can't stand aside and see a potentially meaningful life wasted."

George took her hand and held it reassuringly. "Of course not, but let's give him a chance to solve his own problems. He just might surprise you."

Mary Ann stood up. "It's a fine line, George—helping, but not interfering. We'll both do our best to walk it. But right now I'm just plain tired."

George concurred. "It's been a long day."

Mary Ann called to the dog. "Come on, Christmas—last chance to go outside." Walking to the back door, she turned on the exterior floodlights and let the Lab out into the yard. She watched him for a few minutes as he poked about the yard. His black coat stood out against the white snow, and to her there was something regal about the old dog and the way he carried himself. He stopped and sniffed the night air, aware of some presence or sound lost to human senses.

Mary Ann watched as Christmas moved beneath an old weather vane in the driveway that George and his grandpa Bo had fastened to a steel pole sixty years earlier. It was a small replica of a twin-engine Cessna, swiveling on the pole, charting a new course with each change in the wind's direction, its tiny aluminum props twirling in the moonlight.

Mary Ann opened the door and called out, "Come on, Christmas. Time for bed."

CHAPTER 3

CLOSING A small business is hard—so hard that some ex-proprietors just give the keys to the bank and walk away. Without emotion, strangers can more easily crate broken dreams and set them curbside with the other discarded mementos of failure: reams of ledger paper stained by red ink; the personnel records of downsized employees; marketing brochures for failed products; and all the other pictures, plaques, and trophies of a team that will not suit up to play another day.

While some closings will always be harder than others, closing an animal shelter might be the hardest of all. When your inventory is made up of living, breathing creatures—animals that you have come to love, innocent pets, each human-animal relationship its own untold story—it is tough. If things get really bad, you may well have to destroy the very things you have spent your entire career feeding, caring, loving, and fighting to save.

In the early morning after the town hall meeting, Hayley sat at her desk trying to work through all the levels of this disaster, from the most obvious to the most subtle. Her face rested in cupped hands. She felt clammy, and the acid in her stomach was bubbling and boiling like a witch's cauldron.

She took out a pencil and paper from the top drawer and started to make one of her lists. Trying to get her logical mind around the previous day's events proved an impossible task. The paper remained blank, so she pondered a different approach: a gigantic flowchart on her wall—full of arrows and scribbles—that would miraculously set her a course past the snow-capped peaks that towered in front of her like lofty Kilimanjaro. That didn't work either. She didn't know where to begin because she had not yet fully grasped the problem.

It was only five in the morning, but already she had been sitting at her desk for more than an hour avoiding the hardest part, the first step in any crisis. It can only begin after we have accepted the unacceptable.

She got up and turned on the kennel lights. She walked up and down the aisles between the cages of dogs and cats, now yawning, stretching, and seemingly questioning the early hour and the deviation in their routine. Pacing, stopping in front of every cage, Hayley wondered which ones would make it. What would be the fate of each pair of soft, eager eyes? How could she turn her back on them?

The events of life are supposed to sculpt us, to chip away at us, giving us form. That morning Hayley felt the stone hammer falling unusually hard, without mercy; shards of her old life were scattering in all directions. Intuitively she knew that she couldn't resolve her crisis by trying to go around it. Painful as it might be, the only way was straight through it. Taking a deep breath, she struggled to define what the past ten years had meant to her, while she felt as if the core of her being was splitting into pieces.

Her whole career seemed to be summed up in those precious moments when an owner walked away with a cat or a dog.

Although they operate somewhat like a business, shelters are outside the normal bounds of commerce. When a sale is made, a transaction completed, hearts are transformed and some immeasurable energy—call it love—is set in motion. The shelter in Crossing Trails had improved the lives of so many families, and now all those moments, all those heartfelt transactions, would end forever. No, this wasn't just another business shutting its doors.

Defining the loss brought Hayley closer to the raw nerve of her hurt, but there was more to confront. It was suddenly obvious. The closing of the shelter would be awful for all the lost and abandoned pets in her corner of the world. Yes, that was a huge part of it. The loss to the community of this seemingly bottomless reservoir of companionship and love was tragic. Yes, that too. But the worst part of it might be what she would have to do next, what she was dreading the most. The prospect of speaking words that would hurt another human being caused her immeasurable pain.

In a few hours, she would have to deliver news that might very well derail a young man's life. Not just any young man, but Todd McCray, whom she had come to love and respect like a brother.

The first item on the list that morning was a miserable task. She'd been cast in the role of the city's henchman. Having not tried out for the part, she wondered if she could reject it. Could she just pick up her car keys, walk out the front door, and drive away without looking back? She could picture Todd's face, crestfallen and devastated. She shook her head, back and forth, in disbelief, in anger. It wasn't fair.

Hayley stood up and made the short journey across the room. She lifted the blinds and looked out the window. A hard north wind pushed against the pane and she could feel cold air seeping through the cracked glazing. The sun was rising slowly on a new day. She intentionally bit her lip, once, then again. She was a tough lady. She planned and made lists and flowcharts and still she worried. She believed in action first and emotion second. Still her eyes clouded. The first tear was small, barely perceptible, but the next ones flowed freely down her cheeks. It felt good to cry. It meant that, finally, she had broken through, reached down and touched the deep heart of the matter. She knew what she was losing. Having taken the first steps in accepting her loss, she was now ready to take the first steps to deal with it.

She realized she was feeling overwhelmed because she was taking too much of the burden on her own shoulders and thinking it was her job to fix everything and everyone. It was too much for her—too much for anyone, really. She did not have to take this on all by herself. She could ask for help and move forward as best she could: making her to-do lists and completing each task, one by one. She picked up a clean index card and uncapped her pen. She pushed hard and allowed the ink to pool until she forced herself to write:

1. *Get help,* and below that,
2. *Tell Todd.*

Hayley put the pen down. That was enough for now.

When it came to seeking help, Laura Jordan and Doc Pelot were the first people who came to mind. Both were unpaid volunteers at the shelter and Hayley's good friends. Although they would be upset by the news, they were good, level-headed partners in the shelter business and she could trust them to help her. She also considered calling George and Mary Ann McCray and asking them to help. As much as Todd loved his parents, she also knew him to be a young man trying to find his own space outside the sphere of his parents' care. Getting them involved might be a betrayal of Todd's sovereignty, a step backward for him. She decided to stick with Doc Pelot and Laura. At least for now. She checked the time. It was still a little too early to call them.

After warming her coffee in the microwave, Hayley sat back down with her feet perched on her desk. The idea of getting some help made her feel better. She turned her focus back to Todd. She wondered why, of all the miserable tasks she was facing, telling Todd seemed the worst.

Perhaps it was because she felt responsible for him. She had no confidence that he would survive in the work world without her guidance. She had gladly coached him the last few years, and he had willingly repaid her, with interest, by hard work and an unflinching commitment to the shelter's animals. Todd's talents and the shelter's needs were a good match. She sensed that there would be no other suitable job opportunities for him in Crossing Trails.

Ready to end her ruminating, Hayley checked her watch again. It was 7:15. She decided that it was not too early to call her eighty-two-year-old helper and the county's long-retired veterinarian, Doc Pelot, for advice. Before dialing, she formed a picture in her mind of the man she was hoping could help her. She imagined him sitting in his old vet clinic near his home. He had turned it into his "shop" and escaped there to do all the things that annoyed his wife, like smoking his pipe to his heart's content, playing cards with his dwindling pool of cronies, fixing them gin martinis, arguing politics, and telling them the same old jokes that kept them laughing for hours. He claimed that his vices kept him interesting, to which his wife would quickly respond, "A little too interesting."

Doc Pelot had known Todd and Hayley since they were both children. He was a devout animal lover and had been one of the shelter's founders back in the 1970s. Hayley often turned to Doc Pelot when she was stuck. And she'd never been more stuck than she was that morning.

On the third ring Doc Pelot took the pipe from his mouth, present but not lit at that early hour, and answered the phone, "Pelot."

"Doc, it's Hayley."

"If you're calling to tell me the shelter's closing, don't bother. George McCray already phoned me. It's ridiculous. I thought all the idiots were stashed away in Washington." His voice rose in irritation. "Now I find that a few of them have stayed home in Crossing Trails."

When Doc Pelot finished his rant on politicians, Hayley got to the subject of her call. "What about Todd? I'm not sure how to handle this with him."

Doc Pelot thought patiently and let out a long exasperated breath. "It's going to be hard on him. I'll get dressed and come on over to help you and Todd sort this out."

After she hung up, Hayley realized she was still short on concrete advice, so she decided to call the shelter's other volunteer staffer, Laura Jordan, the nurse's aide who worked at the Crossing Trails Wellness Center. Laura and Todd had been high school classmates, but they hadn't truly become friends until about a year ago after Laura accidentally hit a stray dog with her car. Her first thought was to immediately call her acquaintance from school, knowing that he worked at the shelter. She was so concerned about the animal that she stopped in to visit the shelter daily. With each visit Laura grew closer to her, the young man who cared for her, and the wonderful place that found homes for lost pets.

Ah, Gracie—what a remarkable job Todd had done with the dog, Hayley thought. The white retriever was another in a long series of foreclosure dogs, but from the beginning it had been clear that Gracie had something special to offer. With Doc Pelot's gentle guidance, Todd and Laura had nursed the white retriever back to health one day at a time. Gracie's recovery was miraculous. Within weeks she was fearlessly crawling over Laura and Todd like a six-week-old puppy. She was eager to please and very trainable. Todd began working with her, and soon she had a considerable repertoire of basic obedience skills.

After two months of rehabilitation and training, the inevitable occurred. Even though she was fully recovered, Todd refused to put Gracie into the general shelter population where she could be adopted. He had other plans for her. With minimal cajoling from Todd, Laura—by now a shelter volunteer—adopted Gracie. Todd spent the ensuing months working with Gracie. Todd was always direct. He told Laura, "Some of the things you have a hard time doing, we can teach her to do for you!"

Hayley knew that Laura did yoga every morning to help with her movement and balance. Unless her work schedule at the Wellness Center had to be adjusted, Laura and Gracie volunteered at the shelter on Friday mornings. Even at this early hour, Hayley was confident that Laura would be out of bed. She located her number in the directory on her phone and hit Dial.

"Laura . . . this is Hayley . . . I wanted to talk to you before you came in this morning."

"Sure, what's up?"

"I've got some rotten news that I have to tell you and Todd. I just want you to know what's going on here at the shelter so you have some time to think about it before you come in. Also I may need your help. Did you or your parents hear about what happened at the town hall meeting last night?"

As Hayley communicated all the details of the prospective closing of the shelter, Laura didn't say much in response. Instead, she leaned against the kitchen counter for support and looked down at Gracie. She thought about all the dogs whose lives had been saved over the years and all the dogs whose lives might not be saved once the shelter was closed. She could not imagine life without Gracie's love and assistance. Laura knew that without the shelter, Gracie would not be in her life. In all likelihood the dog wouldn't have had another chance. It would have been such a tragic waste.

"The worst part of it for me may be telling Todd," Hayley was saying. "And that's where I'm going to need your help."

"Don't worry, Hayley, Todd can handle this—I'll be there for him. We all have to get through it together. That's the only way. I'll get dressed and come right over."

CHAPTER 4

WITH CHRISTMAS in tow, Todd made his way back to the shelter's small kitchen space, hung up his coat, and put his lunch in the small refrigerator. Finding Hayley at her desk, he quickly greeted her with a question: "How do you think Christmas did last night in front of all those people?" He nodded his head excitedly up and down, answering his own question. "I thought he did great."

Hayley got up and moved around to the other side of her desk, where she could reach down and scratch Christmas on his gray chin. "No doubt about it. He's a great dog, but you did great, too. It didn't seem to bother you one bit . . . standing up there in front of all those people."

Christmas arched his back and stretched. This was his way of inviting her to extend her scratching to his entire torso. Hayley willingly complied. Christmas turned and looked up at her with green eyes that expressed nothing but gratitude.

"Talking in front of people doesn't bother me. Writing things down—that's what I hate," Todd said.

"Todd, there is something we need to discuss this morning."

Before Hayley could continue, the door to the shelter opened. Laura's voice carried well. "Hello. Todd, are you here?"

"In the back!" he yelled.

Doc Pelot parked his old Chrysler Imperial, which he had a habit of driving too fast, and walked in behind Gracie and Laura. He scratched the white retriever's ears. "I like Gracie's new vest," Doc boomed, as they headed for Hayley's office.

"Thank you," Laura said. "My parents bought it for us."

Todd turned to Hayley and supplied an explanation. "The new vest has a better handle on the top for Laura to grip for balance, and Laura's mom liked the yellow-and-red warning colors better. With the red only, some people still didn't understand that they weren't supposed to pet Gracie when she was working."

Doc, Laura, and Gracie turned the corner into the office space and Hayley greeted them. "Good morning, volunteers. Thanks for coming in."

Doc Pelot muttered to himself.

Hayley tried to break the awkwardness they were feeling. "Looks like the entire team is on hand this morning." She wanted to say what she knew some of the others were thinking. *How sad that we won't be getting together for much longer.*

Todd wondered why everyone was milling about, and he was excited about showing Laura and Doc Pelot some of the newly arrived animals. He asked Hayley, "Should we get to work?"

"Sure, but go on without me. I have some other stuff to do this morning and then I need to talk to everyone."

Hayley sat down at her desk while Todd led Doc Pelot and Laura along the middle aisle of the kennel space. Todd's red Converse tennis shoes squeaked on the linoleum floor. Slightly bent over, Doc Pelot shuffled along behind the others.

Many of the caged dogs grew excited and barked, whined, and even howled at the sight of the humans and of the two canines—Christmas and Gracie—that tagged along. Other dogs sat silent and motionless in their cages, as if they had given up.

Laura pushed a cart of vet supplies and acted as Doc Pelot's assistant as he gave each dog its twice-weekly checkup. Because the dogs and cats were in close proximity it was easier for disease to spread if conditions were not closely monitored. Todd would let each dog out of its cage for Doc Pelot to greet and inspect. It was in movement or lack of it that the vet could quickly surmise an animal's health. When he was convinced each dog was in good shape, he would repeat his mantra, "No sick dog here!"

That morning Laura noticed sadness in his voice. Try as she might, she knew she was mirroring the same sentiment each time she spoke.

After Doc Pelot completed each brief checkup, Todd would enthusiastically ask each animal to *sit* or *stay* or otherwise respond to some basic command. Todd was in charge of exercising each dog, and he also used that time to work with every guest on basic obedience, house-training, or sometimes a special trick, as with the next dog on the tour.

Addressing the entire group, Todd said, "This is Earl. He came in three days ago, and we've already given him his shots." Todd pointed to the young brown pit bull–Lab mix with a tail wagging at the speed of light. "He's real friendly and a good learner. I've already taught him one trick. He's good at it already." Todd removed Earl from his cage and put him in a sitting position so that the vet could give him a good going-over.

Doc Pelot opened the dog's mouth and peered inside. Satisfied, he made some notes on his chart and said, "No sick dog here."

"Watch this." Todd got Earl's attention and then moved his right hand in tight concentric circles as if he were fever-ishly whipping egg whites. Mimicking the hand motion, Earl started to spin around, chasing his tail. When Earl stopped spinning, Todd gave him a small dog treat and an enthusiastic hug. "He's real good at spinning around and going nowhere."

"Then he'd make a good politician," quipped the old vet, still aggravated by his local government and the budget woes that were about to upend the shelter. Doc Pelot noticed that Todd was looking at him curiously. He abruptly moved the entourage down the aisle. "Next!" he commanded.

Christmas lagged behind, walking a little more slowly these days, but seemingly enjoying his duties as senior shelter dog.

Halfway down the second aisle of cages they came upon a particularly lethargic Tibetan Terrier mix named Westin with an ugly abscess on his neck. The infection had spread, and the poor dog was very sick. Westin failed to get up when Doc Pelot tapped his walnut cane against the cage door. Todd also encouraged Westin, but the dog felt too lousy to budge.

Crestfallen, Todd asked, "What's wrong?"

Doc Pelot bent down and examined the infected spot, took the smoldering old pipe from his mouth, and then reassured Todd. "Don't worry, antibiotics will do the trick. You wait and see."

When the animals needed shots or their bandages changed, Doc Pelot often allowed Laura to do his work—regardless of state veterinary regulations. He pointed his cane at the dog. "Laura, please clean off a spot for me and we'll give him a shot." He selected the correct antibiotic on the supply cart and instructed Laura on dosing the syringe.

Todd opened the cage door a bit wider, and Doc Pelot touched the exact spot on the dog's neck so Laura knew where to stick the needle. Bracing herself against Gracie's stable body for extra balance, she cleaned Westin's neck with an alcohol-soaked cotton swab. She placed a gentle hand on the little dog to calm him, and with the other hand she jabbed the dog quickly and confidently.

"Nice job, Laura."

She looked back at the vet. "Dogs are a lot easier to inject than humans."

"Westin will feel better in a few hours. I'll come by and check on him again before I leave."

At the end of the second aisle, several guest cages were reserved for dogs that were not yet eligible for adoption. The shelter gave owners three days to claim a dog before it was moved into the general population. This waiting period also provided Hayley and Todd an opportunity to assess each dog's health and suitability for adoption. If a dog was vicious, it would become an unfortunate exception to the shelter's general policy against euthanasia, but such instances were very rare. Most all dogs and cats could be placed if Hayley and Todd were patient and diligent.

Once moved from the guest cages and into the general kennel area, every dog had ninety days to find an owner. After that, different no-kill options had to be considered so that the shelter did not become inundated with unadopt-able dogs.

After he passed the guest cages, Doc Pelot took a seat in one of the chairs he had strategically placed to facilitate periodic rests. He slowly tipped into the chair like a giant tree upended, and he fixed his blue-gray eyes on the white retriever. He tapped his cane on the concrete to gain Gracie's attention. Gracie approached the old man with considerable dignity. She simply rested her head on his leg. He ran his long wrinkled fingers through her white coat. It felt good. The dog reminded him of why he did what he did. The old man had been around long enough to see many things come and go. Change was part of life. Knowing it didn't make it any easier. He looked up at Todd and shook his head. He grumbled under his breath. "What a rotten deal."

While the others made their rounds, Hayley gathered up a pile of photographs—each a shot of a recently adopted dog and its happy new owner. For the last few holidays, she had collected an entire year of adoption photos and used them to decorate the shelter's Christmas tree. They called it their memory tree. She thumbed through the last few placements and experienced a heavy feeling in her gut, so she put the pictures down and exited the side door to collect her thoughts. A few of the recent arrivals were running freely about the fenced yard so Hayley could see how well they interacted with other dogs. While smoking a cigarette, a habit she had unsuccessfully tried to break, Hayley looked to the horizon, hoping some answer might float across the gray winter sky, riding on the back of a distant cloud. As much as she dreaded it, she decided it was time to get the deed over with. She felt a nervous twitch in her right eyelid. It happened rarely, but she knew it as a telltale sign of avoidance and dread. She stomped the cigarette out on the ground and watched the last little wisp of smoke drift aloft. It wasn't going to get any easier.

She resolutely gripped the doorknob, turned it, and walked inside to join the others as they chatted with Doc Pelot in the corridor.

Todd was the first to see her. "Hey."

"Hey, Todd."

Todd wondered if something was wrong. It seemed that Hayley had been avoiding them all morning. "How are you doing?" he asked, frowning.

"I'm dealing with some bad news. Are you up to hearing about it?"

"Sorta," he answered uncomfortably, pulling Christmas closer to him, wondering how anyone could ever be in the mood to hear bad news.

Hayley took it from the beginning. "Last night, after work, the city manager asked me to come by the town hall before the meeting to talk with him and Mayor McDaniel." She took a deep breath and tried to look directly into Todd's eyes, but she couldn't. "The city of Crossing Trails and the county can't fund our shelter anymore. Nobody has enough money, so they decided to shut us down after the first of the year. We have to close. We can't accept any more dogs, and we have to quickly place the ones we still have— no exceptions."

"What she's trying to say," Doc Pelot added, his voice on the edge of cracking, "is that we're going out of business— just like the video rental store and the bakery."

Even with Doc's translation, Todd was confused, but he

could tell from the expressions on the faces of those around him that this was not good news.

"I don't understand. What will our jobs be if we don't take care of the dogs?"

Todd's question hit her like a jab to the gut, and Hayley knew there would be many more painful questions to follow. "We won't have jobs, Todd. That's part of what I'm saying."

"What?" Todd's face fell as his eyes grew wide. "Can they do that?"

"I think so," Hayley answered.

"Maybe we should talk to a lawyer," Todd said. "I dog-sit for one—Susan Reeves. She might be able to tell the mayor that they can't close the shelter. . . . Where will the dogs live? Where will we work?"

Hayley tried to stay calm, but it was difficult. She was cycling back and forth between anger and sadness, and it felt like someone had sucked the air right out of her. She struggled to get her words out. "Todd, there is no law that says that the city or the county must operate a shelter for our dogs or give us jobs. That's the way it is."

"Well, it's not fair, and Susan Reeves told me that lawyers try to make things fair." It had been years, but Todd was experiencing that hopeless feeling that he'd had in algebra or history when he was called on in class and didn't know the answer. He had wanted to run away from it all. Yet this was different. He didn't care about algebra or history; he cared about these dogs. His breathing became labored, as if he had just sprinted around the block. He looked at each of his friends and finally spoke. "We have to do something. This isn't right."

Laura shook her head. "I don't think there is anything we can do about it."

"I don't understand. Aren't dogs important?"

"Yes, Todd, they're important."

Todd stood and began to pace back and forth, stabbing at the floor with his red tennis shoes. He considered another trusted resource. "How about Brenda Williams at Channel Six? She is the 'Problem Solver.'" Todd and Brenda had first met several years earlier when she did a story about the shelter's Adopt a Dog for Christmas program. It turned out that Brenda Williams took the plight of lost pets seriously. Even though Cherokee County was on the fringes of its viewing area, the TV station ran a great story that helped dramatically spike seasonal fostering and adoption.

Laura took Todd's hand and gently pulled him back into his chair. "I know they did that story on the Christmas dogs, but I think the Problem Solver is more for people who buy bad cars and can't get their money back. But you can try her if you think it'll help. Who knows?"

Hayley sighed. She knew she had to see this conversation with Todd through to its conclusion. "Todd, you and I will have to start looking for new jobs. Any of our dogs that we can't place will have to be transferred to different shelters. I'm sorry. I don't like it, but there doesn't seem to be anything I can do about it. We're just going to have to help each other get through this."

Hayley knew that she needed to find some way to comfort Todd—that the circumstances must seem overwhelming to him. She was not expecting what happened next.

Frightened and anxious as he was, Todd tried to shift his focus away from himself and the dogs. "I'm sorry, Hayley. I know you love our dogs and cats. It's not your fault."

"Thanks for understanding. That's a big help to me."

"It's still not fair," Todd added.

"I know. I've never lost a job before."

"Me either. This is the only one I've ever had."

Todd shook his head. Once more he pulled Christmas close to him for comfort, feeling the animal's strength and love. He tried to draw from it. "Where will all the new dogs go?"

Hayley watched the two of them together for a few seconds, and it occurred to her just how lucky Todd was to have the old Lab by his side. She suspected that the dog might be far more helpful to Todd than Hayley could ever hope to be. "I don't know, Todd. We'll have the weekend to think about it. Next week we'll see what we can figure out."

Still holding Todd's hand, Laura gave it a gentle squeeze. And then she did it again. And again. And again.

Todd didn't seem to notice, but she was pressing a message into his hand: *We'll get through this. Together.*

CHAPTER 5

LATER THAT same day, Todd put his jacket and gloves on, opened the back door of his small cabin, and called Christmas to follow him. Many years earlier, before his parents had bought it as a rental property, the cabin had been owned by a man named Thorne, and to this day George still often referred to Todd's place as Thorne's cabin. A year earlier, as a step in fostering Todd's independence, George and Mary Ann had allowed Todd to move into it.

Todd had a favorite trail that he had walked on since he was a little boy. It led west past his parent's house—just a few hundred yards away from Thorne's cabin—and then turned south through a twenty-acre meadow that was lined with scrub cedar. Eventually, he could amble down along Kill Creek for miles on end. Today he had a destination in mind.

Todd had a favorite spot beneath a giant sycamore, and near a creek crossing, where he felt grounded. For generations the McCray family had gathered there on the banks of the creek to enjoy one another's company. An old picnic table was chained to a tree so it wouldn't be swept away in high water. Not far from the table were two sturdy hickory trees. A rope hammock was suspended between them, and lawn chairs waited patiently for spring's arrival, tied down in the crook of the westernmost tree.

Todd wiped the snow off the bench seat of the picnic table and sat down. He could see the footprints where little squirrels had tracked across the snow on the tabletop. Walnut remnants suggested that the table had not gone without use.

Within a few minutes, and with just a little effort, he could hear from warmer and distant times the laughter, the shouting, the splashing in the water that had punctuated so many hours spent on this hallowed family ground. He could feel his father's strong arms, gripping one of his little-boy legs in one hand and an arm in another, playfully swinging him over the surface of the cool creek water on a hot August afternoon. As Todd's body dipped just beneath the surface of the water like a little hawk chasing a frog, his mother would shout, "George, be careful with him! He's not a skipping stone!"

The old Lab's whine brought Todd's attention back to the present. The dog wagged his bushy tail for attention. Todd took off his gloves and dug his fingers down into the dark, warm fur of the Lab. He pulled Christmas closer for comfort and let the dog steady him. Today Todd felt like he had been knocked to the ground by a giant playground bully. He was just dazed enough that he needed to get his bearings before he could get back up on his feet. Without understanding how or why, he drew solace from the dog and this spot on the creek.

He wondered if perhaps this was why Hayley had wanted him to take the rest of the day off, so he could try to get back on his feet. After Laura and Doc Pelot had left the shelter, he and Hayley had sat down together for lunch. She asked him, "Have you ever wondered what you would do if you didn't work here?" as she pulled the last potato chip from the bag they were sharing.

Todd thought for a very long time, so long that it started to make them both feel uneasy, before he finally answered, "I didn't know that someday I might not work here."

She reached across the small old Formica table and put her hand on Todd's forearm. "I understand. Why don't you take the rest of the day off and really give it some thought? What do you want to do?"

"Hayley, I don't know. We only have a few days left here at the shelter, and we have a lot of work to do for these dogs." He pointed in the direction of the kennel.

"Understood. But Todd, give it some thought, okay? What do you want to do?"

Todd just looked at Hayley and didn't say a word. Still, he knew she was right. He needed to think. In the end he followed her suggestion and left an hour early.

Todd got up from the picnic table and walked the short

distance to the bank of the creek. Water trickled more than flowed down Kill Creek as it made its way around occasional patches of ice and snow. Todd tossed black walnut shells into the water. In his younger days, the black Lab would have dashed into the water and made a great game of attacking and retrieving the walnuts. Now he was content to sit on the bank and watch the walnut shells bob up and down and slowly float away.

"What do I really want to do?" Todd asked himself out loud. It seemed like a strange question. "Does that make any sense to you, Christmas?"

The dog looked up at him with eager eyes that seemed to say, Don't worry. I love you and that's all that really matters.

What do you really want to do, Todd? He'd heard that before. It was the kind of question that teachers asked him in high school. When he shared his aspirations, they would say, "Todd, you're not being realistic." That was what they said, but he knew what they meant. *Todd, you have disabilities. You can't do things like everyone else. You're not smart. Remember?*

When Todd told Mary Ann what he thought his guidance counselors or teachers were saying about him, she warned him, "Don't be so sure about what other people are thinking about you." Still, he was pretty sure on this one. His teachers didn't seem to have much confidence in him. As Todd got older and better able to reflect on his disability, his mother also told him that on the other side of every deficit is a corresponding strength. "Todd, it's true, there are things you can't do as well as some, but there are also things you are so much better at than me, your dad, or about anyone else I know." It was a simple little message, but it was repeated often enough and convincingly enough that it kept Todd confident enough to take the chances in life that must be taken to live fully. Mary Ann meant every word of it. To her, Todd was more, not less; fuller and richer in the aspects of life that really matter. It was as if the special elixir that was Todd had been delivered in a cracked crucible. That was the trade-off. She forever felt the need to hold him close to protect the container. No matter how far apart they might be in the years ahead, he would always feel that closeness.

That afternoon, sitting on the bank of the creek, he thought about what he had told his teachers five years earlier when they'd asked what he wanted to do, and his face flushed with embarrassment. Singer on *American Idol*, jet pilot, and crime-scene investigator. He smiled and said to himself, "No wonder they thought I was dumb!"

The one thing he liked to do more than anything else was work with animals, especially dogs. Everybody knew that. Yet there was nowhere in Crossing Trails where he could do that but at the shelter. He wondered why everyone was so worried about his finding a job. It seemed to him that their first priority should be the dogs and cats at the shelter.

He also thought about Laura and how much fun he'd had with her over the past months. Much of their time together had been spent at the shelter on the Fridays when she volunteered. That would end soon. It was unclear to Todd how he would continue to find time to be with her. Over the last few months it seemed that every week he had been counting down the days till Friday when he could see her. Now what would he look forward to? He loved old Doc Pelot like the grandfather he never had. Without the shelter, when would he see him? Hayley was like a sister and a boss all rolled into one. Todd didn't like the idea of all these wonderful people having a diminished role in his life. He didn't like the idea of pets with no place to go.

He nudged Christmas with the palm of his hand, a little signal that meant it was time to move on. The two of them started to walk back toward home. When they got even with the McCray barn, Todd turned north and made a path toward his dad's little office in the barn. It was the slow winter months for a farmer, so it was likely he would find George puttering about the barn.

Todd pushed the barn door open and found his father polishing an old cowbell at his desk.

It had been a pleasant afternoon project for George. When he had been a boy, it had been his job to rise early in the morning, climb on his horse, and herd straggling cows up to the barn for milking. The cowbells made it easier to locate the wanderers. Herding the cows was very hard work for a boy. After George's father died, the work got even harder. For five generations now, the McCray family had found something very rewarding about spilling their sweat and blood onto that bit of Kansas farm ground. Their hard work had paid off, bringing good times for the McCray family. It was difficult for George to accept that the family farm might one day come to an end.

"What's that?" Todd asked when his dad looked up.

George put the rusted bell down and turned the grinder motor off. "Just an old cowbell I found buried out in the feedlot. It's from one of the milk cows, back when your great-grandfather Bo and I had the dairy together. I thought it might be fun to polish it up. Don't see many of these around today." Christmas moved toward George and offered a tail-wagging doggie greeting. George reached down and patted the old Lab on the head. "Christmas, how was your day?"

As Todd was apt to do, he got right to the point. "It was a bad day for us and for a bunch of cats and dogs, too. They're going to close the shelter." He looked down at his red Converse tennis shoes. "I don't know what to do now. I guess we have to find another way to rescue all those dogs and cats, and I have to find a new job doing something else."

"Son, these days are bound to arrive whether we like it or not. Women, work, and hemorrhoids are a man's greatest challenges. Pull up that stool and we'll talk about it."

George and Mary Ann had spent the entire last evening, after the town hall meeting, preparing for this inevitable conversation with Todd about the closing of the shelter.

George generally was of the opinion that the best way to foster Todd's march toward total independence was to leave him alone just like he had done with his other four adult children. If they asked for a helping hand, he gave it. If they didn't ask for it, that was fine, too. This was George's way of showing that he respected their ability to make their own choices and to learn from their own mistakes, just like he had. He liked the motto *If you're not making mistakes, it means you're not trying hard enough.* It's the getting up again—after the toddler falls—that eventually makes young legs strong enough to walk on. George was not worried about Todd stumbling, not before and not now.

Mary Ann felt differently. Her primal need to protect her children was amplified with Todd. She worried that he was too fragile to sustain life's dings and drops. It was hard for her to watch him tumble and not rush out, pillow in hand, to break the fall. She thought that caring and loving parenting naturally entailed gentle and distant supervision so that Todd did not have to scale dangerous obstacles that were too tall for him to overcome. She could not help wondering why George simply did not recognize that Todd was not like their other children.

"And if you keep treating him differently," George had retorted, "Todd won't have a chance to ever catch up and be his own man."

Over the years they had tried to find a middle ground when they could. George thought Todd should move into

Crossing Trails and have a place of his own. Todd seemed ready to manage his own money, time, and living arrangements. Mary Ann thought he was doing perfectly fine living upstairs with them—as he always had and she hoped he always would. They had compromised and moved Todd down the hill and into Thorne's cabin.

As with many compromises, neither parent was totally satisfied. Mary Ann found it harder to keep an eye on Todd, to help him when he needed it. She found that she worried more when she was not in touch with him and his needs, the way she always had been. In her opinion, his cabin was always a mess and his eating habits were poor. George pointed out that in that regard Todd was hardly different from any other young man living on his own for the first time. But Mary Ann was concerned about more than Todd's housekeeping abilities; she worried that he was lonely and isolated by himself.

For his part, George wanted Todd to start experiencing life without parental monitoring. In his mind, Todd's considerable progress the last few years had been a direct result of his accepting adult responsibilities, including having a job and a home of his own. George was not inclined to rescue Todd from his current predicament, at least not without giving him a chance to work through it first on his own. Mary Ann wanted to assure Todd that he was not alone in this world, that together his parents could make things right for him.

For now, George and Mary Ann didn't have to agree. Each would talk to him in their own way.

❄

Todd pulled the stool over by his father and sized up the problem. "We have to find a new place for a whole lot of dogs and cats before the end of the year. That's not much time."

"You're pretty good at finding homes for pets. You'll make it happen."

"I don't know, Dad. It gets harder every year. Hayley says it's because of the economy. We only found twelve adoption families last December. I'm not sure we can do any better than that this year."

"Is there something else you have to do besides find homes for all those critters?" George asked.

"I have to find a job for me."

George picked up the old bell and rang it gently. "Good answer. How are you planning on doing that?"

"That's what I wanted to talk to you about. Hayley says I need to think about what I want to do for the rest of my life. I want to work with dogs, and the shelter is the only place where I can do that." Saying the words made Todd feel closed in as if he were cornered and without options. He put it into words as best he could. "So it's like I'm stuck in the mud on the tractor. My wheels are just spinning."

George had thought about this all day. He wasn't a big fan of the follow-your-dream mentality. He thought it bordered on self-indulgence and was not a practical approach for Todd. "Todd, let me ask you something. When you are really hungry, do you sit around and think about what you would like to eat, or do you go look in the refrigerator and grab what's there?"

That one was easy. "I'd go into the fridge and hope there was something I like a lot. Ice cream would be good."

"There you go! Well, finding work is the same thing, really. You'll never get anywhere by just thinking about what might be perfect for you. You've got to find what's out there and make it happen. If there is no ice cream in the fridge, you might have to make yourself a peanut butter and jelly sandwich. Does that make sense?"

"Or maybe I get in the car, drive to the store, and buy ice cream?"

George had to admit Todd had him on that one, so he tried again. "Todd, if you go into a restaurant do you order what's on the menu or do you tell them what sounds good to you?"

"You have to order off the menu." Todd reached down and nervously petted his dog. He knew his dad was trying to reach out to him and help him understand something that was resting just beyond his grasp. He knew his dad was doing this in the most patient and loving way he could, but what he was saying was still not sinking in.

"See, Todd, you've got to go out there and find out what

jobs are available. That's like the food on the menu or the food you have in the refrigerator. Sitting around thinking about where you wish you could work is like the food in your mind. You can't eat food in your mind. Thinking about food doesn't fill you up. Does it?"

It clicked in a vague way. Todd translated what his dad was saying to mean that thinking alone wouldn't get him a job. That much made sense. He walked over to his dad and hugged him. "Thanks, Dad. I think I understand now why my wheels were spinning."

"Trust me, Todd. You're not the first person to get their wheels spinning on this one. I'm always hearing about someone's kid going off to college or trade school to study their dream—poetry, cliff dwellers, or something that sounds real interesting—and then they get home and act surprised when they can't find work. They have it all backwards. We have to find out who is hiring, what work is out there in the world, and then get trained to do it."

George handed Todd a copy of *The Prairie Star.* He folded the paper back to the classified section and then spread it out on his makeshift desk. "Come over here a minute and look at this."

Todd looked over his father's shoulder and George continued, "These are the jobs in town, where people need help. This is the list you've got to pick from. It's like the job menu. Because the economy is weak now, there aren't a lot of openings. But whether we like it or not, this is what's on the job menu. Take it and look it over. See what's out there.

It might be you have to work at something less than perfect for a while."

Todd took the paper from his dad. "Thanks, I'll look it over."

"I circled a few that might be worth checking into."

Todd turned toward the barn door and started to leave. "See you later, Dad. Thanks for your help." Todd looked down at Christmas and asked, "You coming along or staying?"

George and Mary Ann were amused by the way Christmas wandered back and forth between Thorne's cabin and their farmhouse. Today, Christmas seemed content on the floor beneath George's feet. Tomorrow, he might spend the day with Todd. At times he would paw on the door of either home, and when let out, he would travel across the narrow meadow that separated the two dwellings, seemingly ready to spend time at his other place.

The old Lab's tail swept back and forth several times, but he did not get up as Todd got ready to leave the barn, so Todd buttoned up his coat, put on his blue stocking cap, and said, "I guess he's staying."

It was cold enough for Todd to walk briskly down McCray's Hill. From a distance, Thorne's cabin had a rustic appeal, but it was a simple place: only one big room with a kitchen at the back and a bedroom and small bath to the side. Once inside, Todd hung his coat on a peg and went through his mail. He found a plate of his favorite cookies on the kitchen table with a note from his mom.

Todd—Sorry about the shelter closing. I know you're worried about the dogs. I'll be home tonight. Why don't you come by so we can talk it over? We'll get through this together! We love you!!!

Mom

Todd set the note down on the table, gobbled down a cookie, and checked the cell phone he had left on the kitchen table with his car keys. There was a message. He pushed the little symbol for a tape and the speaker button so he could hear it play while he ate his cookies. He heard a female voice. "Todd, it's Laura. I could use some more help setting out Christmas decorations tonight. Can you come by around seven?" Todd crammed down another cookie and called Laura back. He'd be there.

Todd hung up the phone and quickly called Mary Ann to thank her and let her know that he would be helping Laura for the second night in a row. Although disappointed, she understood. "Drive carefully, Todd, and we'll talk later."

After she hung up, she tried to piece together the aggravatingly cryptic summary George had given her of his conversation with Todd: "I gave him the Help Wanted section of the paper. He's going to read it. That's enough for now. Give him a chance to work it out."

CHAPTER 6

THE WEEKEND was spent doing very little. Both Hayley and Todd felt like they were going to walk up to the mirror and see someone else staring back at them, as if they had been handed a new identity. Monday they were still in such a fog that they found it hard to do much more than wander around asking each other the same question and getting the same answer.

"How are you doing?"

"Lousy. How about you?"

"Same."

After work, Todd went over to Laura's house so she could help him with his résumé. Over Todd's objections, Hayley insisted that this was the first step in finding employment. Laura's father turned over his office so they could use his computer and printer. With Christmas at his feet, Todd sat at the computer and pecked away at the keyboard. His typing was acceptable—his texting skills were even better—but he needed help with grammar and spelling. Laura sat beside him, with Gracie at her feet, and proofread his work. The two dogs were side-by-side. Gracie would try to entice Christmas into playing with her by playfully nipping at his paws. The black Lab would patiently shift his paws away from Gracie and then place one paw on her head to remind the much younger dog that his days of roughhousing were behind him.

Because there was an error or two on virtually every line, it took Todd and Laura over an hour to get a draft together. When they were finished, Laura printed out a clean copy for closer inspection.

"This is good!" Laura said. "I'd hire you."

Todd got up from the office chair and paced about the room as if he had been granted a pardon from a life sentence. He sighed with relief at having the dreaded résumé task behind him. He'd spent years in high school barely passing any class that involved writing skills. He had no desire to relive those difficult times—even for one evening. He sat down on the floor next to Christmas and held the dog close to him. He liked being at Laura's house. This was one of the few times they had been alone together. He wished they were doing anything but writing a résumé. Even so, Laura's helping him list his accomplishments validated his skills, and he was happily surprised at what he had learned about himself in the process.

Laura had a knack for taking the ordinary tasks that Todd did, day in and day out, and making them sound significant. He read and re-read the paragraph on his current position. It sounded pretty impressive.

> ASSISTANT SHELTER MANAGER—responsible for caring for, grooming, and feeding over fifty cats and dogs. Developed innovative strategies and processes for promoting high adoption rates at nationally recognized shelter. Highest rating on all employee reviews.

"Laura?" Todd asked.

She looked up. "Yes?"

"Do you think I will be able to find somewhere to work in Crossing Trails?" She didn't answer right away, so he asked again, "Do you think anyone will hire me?"

Laura knew the market was tough. "Todd, I think lots of people would hire you if they had work. I don't know how many people have jobs to fill right now. That's the problem. If I had an opening, I would hire you and Christmas first thing."

Todd yawned, closed his eyes, and without thinking about it rested his head on Laura's shoulder. Résumé writing was exhausting. "I'm tired."

"I don't like it that you have to drive so far to get home."

Todd opened his eyes. "Ten miles is not that far."

"In that old truck of yours, it's too far to be driving, especially at night." Laura snuggled in closer to Todd. "I miss you when you're out there in that old cabin. It seems so very far away. Like a whole other world."

Todd felt something building in his chest, a mixture of happiness and sadness. He nudged Laura playfully. "Thanks for helping me on my résumé."

Laura grinned sheepishly. "You just needed a little help describing what a great guy you are and what a wonderful employee you would be."

Todd held up the finished résumé proudly. "I better go."

He extended his hand, offering to help Laura up from the sofa. She considered telling him that he needed to walk himself out to his truck. Her arthritis was flaring up and she was feeling tired. She hesitated and looked up at Todd. Pushing through the pain, she said, "Thanks, but Gracie and I can do it ourselves. We need the exercise and the practice. Watch and see what she has learned, thanks to you."

She leaned over and called Gracie to her side. Snapping her vest around her was Gracie's signal that she was on duty for Laura. Laura then gave the "stand" command that Todd had taught the dog to help Laura get up from a chair, because getting down was not the problem. Laura needed to brace her weight against the dog to push herself up from the sofa.

It's quite difficult for some dogs to stay firmly put

while someone seems to be leaning against them, as if pushing them away. In the beginning Gracie had been confused and Todd couldn't figure out the best way to help her, so he Googled the names on the dog-training videos that he had studied and came up with the phone numbers of some of the leading service-dog trainers in the country. When it came to picking up the phone, even as a young boy, Todd had had no reservations. Over the ensuing months Todd developed a long-distance phone relationship with several of the finest service-dog trainers in the business. It had taken several weeks of intensive work and a few training tips, but now Gracie was a pro at helping Laura up.

When Laura gave the command "stand," Gracie positioned her body sideways in front of Laura like a four-legged stool. The dog splayed her feet slightly and braced herself. Laura placed one hand on Gracie's haunches and the other close to her neck, where the dog's front legs could better support Laura's weight. She tilted her torso over the top of the dog's body and then with her palms down, pushed herself up. "Good girl, Gracie."

Once up, she took Todd's elbow in her right hand. "I'll walk you out."

Todd and Laura went out the front door, with their two dogs tagging along. There was no moon, and the stars were crisp and bright. They stood together by the cab of Todd's truck while the engine warmed up. Laura stuck her hands in Todd's coat pockets to keep them warm.

As if on cue, Todd's phone rang. He checked the caller

ID, sighed, and showed Laura the phone, letting Mary Ann's call go to voice mail. "Sometimes my mom loves me too much."

She turned away from Todd and took a step toward her house. "Come on, Gracie. Todd has to get going on that long drive home," she said, rolling her eyes in a teasing way. "Will you call me later, so I don't worry about you being eaten up by all those coyotes I always hear howling out there?"

Todd laughed. "Coyotes don't eat people."

"Are you sure?" she asked.

"Nah, you're thinking of wolves."

Laura growled, "Rrrrff. See you tomorrow."

She reached down, grabbed the handle on Gracie's vest, and made her way back toward the small ranch home where she had lived her entire life. As she reached the front door, Laura turned and waved good-bye to Todd as he pulled off. She stood for a moment and listened to the sound of the poorly muffled truck fade away in the distance.

On the edge of town, Todd checked his messages on his cell phone. His mother still wanted him to stop by and check in with her before he went to bed or, if he was too tired, before he went to work the next morning. The second message was the one he had been hoping for. Brenda Williams—the Problem Solver—asked Todd to call her back tomorrow morning. "Yes!" he said aloud, feeling as if he'd scored a small victory.

Todd drove under a clear sky crowded with stars, the

ground beside the road covered in snow. In the distance, Todd saw a doe in his headlights. He watched it amble across the road. He tapped the brakes and slowed to make sure she reached the other side safely. Once she was across, he switched his foot back to the accelerator and continued on his way to his parents' home.

At the end of his parent's gravel driveway he turned off the ignition. "Come on, Christmas. We're home." The dog lumbered along behind Todd as he entered the family house through the back door.

George and Mary Ann were waiting for him in the living room. Earlier that day, George had cut a Christmas tree from the wild cedars that flanked Kill Creek, and he had set it up in the living room, but the lights and ornaments were still stacked in boxes for another day. Mary Ann, sitting on the sofa knitting a blanket for one of her grandchildren, got up and hugged Todd. George greeted him with a military salute from his recliner by the fire. Todd proudly unfolded the piece of paper that he had painstakingly prepared and handed it to his father before sinking into the sofa. "I already did my résumé, and Laura said it was excellent."

While George looked over the résumé, Christmas strolled over to the fire and rested on the floor with his back to the heat. Exhausted from the day's activities, he quickly fell asleep. George handed the résumé back to Todd. Judging by the glow on his face, he was proud of his son. "Pretty impressive, I'd say."

Todd seemed pleased with himself. "I'm pretty good, aren't I?"

Mary Ann came over and dropped a kiss on Todd's head. "You're the best!"

"Thanks, Mom." Todd was getting his mind around the problem to the point where he could at least sum up the issues for his parents. "I have to find a new job and a new place for our dogs and cats to live, too. Hayley and I are working on the dogs." Todd smiled affectionately as he looked at George. "And Dad gave me the job menu."

George gently corrected Todd. "It's called 'Help Wanted' and it's part of the paper's classified ads section. It's kind of like a menu, but for jobs, not food."

Mary Ann sat down next to Todd. "Your dad and I were talking, and we want you to know that you always have a place here with us on the farm, either in our house or in Thorne's cabin." Christmas began letting out little dog snores.

George added his own thoughts. "What your mom is saying is that we don't want you to worry. We have confidence that you will work it out. You'll get through this. It may take some time. We all need to be patient."

Todd got up from the sofa and sat down next to Christmas so that he too could feel the warmth of the fire on his back. "Thanks, Dad, but I think I'll find something soon. Depending on what I find, I might want to move into Crossing Trails."

Christmas's snoring grew louder. Todd rubbed the old Lab's ears.

Mary Ann set down her knitting. "I don't understand what you mean."

A look came over Todd's face as if he suspected he had said more than he should have. "Depends on where I get a job. It might be easier for me to live in Crossing Trails, you know, closer to work."

A year earlier when Todd had asked about moving into town, living in Thorne's cabin had been a compromise. George could feel Todd's growing aspirations for independence running straight into Mary Ann's often fierce desire to protect her son from a world she feared would not treat him well. He tried to shut the discussion down before either side got entrenched in an indefensible position. "Todd, let's not worry about where you're going to live right now. Once you know where you're working then we'll discuss it."

His mother added, "We like it that you live out here, near us."

"I know." Todd put his hands in his pockets and looked at his parents and his boyhood home. The closing of the shelter was naturally causing Todd to think about things he had never been required to consider. Bit by bit his notion of where and how he best fit into the world was shifting. Over the last year or so, particularly since he had moved into Thorne's cabin and grown closer to Laura, Todd had begun to distinguish his home from his parents' home. Moving back in with his parents would not be a move in the right direction. He wanted to move forward.

Todd turned to George and Mary Ann and said, "I'm going back to my cabin." He leaned over and patted the old sleeping Lab on his head. "Good night, Christmas."

Todd got in his truck and drove down the hill. Once inside his cabin, he turned on the evening news so he could catch his favorite segment on the *Channel Six News:* Brenda Williams, the Problem Solver. There was no cable service in this rural part of Kansas, but Todd had splurged on a satellite dish and with it he got three "local" channels from over a hundred miles away in Kansas City. Most of his attention was on national fare, like Animal Planet (and whatever else he could find that focused on dog training or care), but in the evenings he liked the ritual of watching the local news from the big city down the road.

Channel Six also made shelters and dog rescue a recurring focus of their programming. Every year Todd particularly enjoyed watching their twenty-four-hour Labor Day Pet-a-thon.

Tonight there was the story of an elderly woman who had given a contractor five hundred dollars as a down payment for six thermal replacement windows. The contractor promised to install them before colder weather arrived. After numerous calls that went unanswered, he was still a no-show. Brenda Williams tracked down the contractor, stuck the camera in his face, and demanded an explanation. The camera then cut to a shot of the elderly woman's home the next morning, showing the contractor hard at work installing the windows. The woman had a big smile on her face. Dramatic music played and a deep booming voice proclaimed, "Problem solved!"

Todd was very impressed and loudly mimicked the slogan to the four walls of his cabin. "Problem solved!"

At the next advertisement he texted Laura. "Home safe!" He would call her first thing in the morning. He opened the voice notes application on his phone and dictated a message to himself, "Call Brenda!" He then set a reminder bell for 9:30 the next morning. He figured that even a city lady who slept late would be up by then.

CHAPTER 7

ON CUE Todd's cell phone sounded at 9:30 the next morning and he called Brenda Williams to tell her about the plight of the shelter. She was stunned.

"Todd, that is awful. How could they do that to your shelter? I guess dogs can't vote, so I shouldn't be surprised."

"I think it's about money," Todd added.

"It always is. I'm afraid that raising adequate tax money for the town and the county is a big challenge, even for the Problem Solver."

"Can you do anything about it?"

"Maybe we need to stage a good old-fashioned doggy sit-in. We can bring the dogs, spread newspapers out on the floor of the town hall, and after a few days of *accidents*, maybe they'll give in!"

Todd thought this was funny and laughed at the image in his head. "I like it. Do you think it'll work?"

"Probably not, but let me think on it some more and I'll get back to you in a day or two with something more realistic."

❄️

Late that morning Laura made Todd and Hayley lunch and brought it by the shelter to cheer them up. She included a few brightly decorated Christmas cookies that one of the nurses had brought into the Wellness Center. She went into the break room, put their lunches on the table, and tuned the radio to one of the local stations that played holiday music all day long. "Come on, guys," she proclaimed, "let's get a little holiday spirit going here! It's Christmas in Crossing Trails!"

Hayley playfully grabbed the proffered lunch and growled, "Bah humbug!" and returned to her desk to answer e-mails.

Laura remained with Todd in the small break room and talked with him while he ate. With Christmas and Gracie beside them, they tried to get their minds around the challenges before them.

"How many résumés have you sent out?" Laura asked.

"Seven. I applied for all the jobs in the classified section of the paper that were a fit for me. Hayley helped me send them out this morning. My dad circled some and Hayley found a few more for me. She says if they like my résumé, they might call me in for an interview."

"Which ones sounded the best to you?"

"The one that sounded best was at Paradise Valley Farms. It's that big dairy that's not too far away from here, and I could work with cows. They're not as much fun as dogs, but I still like cows. The one that sounded the worst was the housekeeper at Bargain Beds Motel."

The picture in Laura's mind of Todd tidying up and changing linens caused her to smile for a second, but she realized there was no humor in the situation. These days it was so hard for even the most qualified candidates to find employment. For Todd, finding a job might be a nearly impossible task. She knew that every opening would have a large pool of applicants. What reasonable chance did he have?

"I'm going to miss working here," Todd said.

"I know you will, Todd. I'm going to miss volunteering and seeing you, Hayley, and Doc Pelot."

Todd didn't want Laura to see the hurt and worry on his face, so he leaned down to pet the dogs.

Laura caught the sadness in the air. She removed her phone from her purse. "Todd, I want to work on our calendars."

Todd looked up a bit startled.

Laura continued, "We've got a lot going on, and things are going to get crazy around here if we don't get organized.

I want to make sure neither of us misses the important stuff. Let's sync our phones."

Todd was remarkably competent with his cell phone. His fingers moved adroitly between its myriad functions. By pushing the icon that looked like the page from on old-fashioned flip calendar, he opened the calendar app. He looked up at her. "I'm ready."

"Today is Tuesday, December tenth, and this Friday, at our normal staff meeting, we need a game plan for finding about fifty dogs and cats a home in less than three weeks."

Todd checked his calendar. He already had Friday's meeting down. "I've got it."

"Good, now that same Friday we're going out for an early dinner. You and me only. It's Dutch."

Although unsure about Dutch food, Todd still liked the idea. He looked blankly at his calendar for December 13. There was nothing entered. He wondered how he had missed the event. "I didn't have that down."

Laura was trying to stare into Todd's eyes. She waited for him to notice. When he did, she reached out and rested her hand softly on his. When she was sure she had his attention, she clutched his hand and finished the thought. "You didn't have it down, because I just made the date. Now we are going to make some more dates. I'm going to be here for you, Todd, whether you work at the shelter or not."

When Todd caught on, he blushed, his face hot and cool at the same time. "Thanks, Laura. Let's make some dates."

"Here is another one for you. Next Wednesday, December 18, my mom and dad would like you to go Christmas caroling with us. Put that one down."

"I'm putting it down, Laura," Todd said. "I'm putting it down."

CHAPTER 8

IN THE early afternoon, many patients napped, and with their patient census low, things slowed down at the Wellness Center. Laura and Gracie found themselves with an hour of unscheduled time and wandered down the halls. They ended up at the door of one of their favorite patients, Hank Fisher. Laura looked inside to see if he was awake. Hank immediately lit up at the sight of the duo.

"Come on in and see me!"

Laura's legs had started to bother her, and when that happened the pain often radiated up into her hips. Still, she never complained. "Do you mind if I sit?"

Hank motioned to a chair. "Please do."

Hank had suffered a series of ongoing heart problems and had contracted a bad case of the flu. He was stubborn about not getting the rest he needed, so they had put him in the hospital, where he had no other choice. Hank's wife had died earlier in the summer.

Because Hank lived just down the road from the McCray farm, George was helping with his chores while he was in the hospital. Hank and Doc Pelot were also longtime friends. They were the only survivors of the group that had helped establish the shelter many years ago, and they had remained close friends ever since. Doc Pelot admiringly described Hank as the "money man." While Hank scoffed at the notion of a dairy farmer having money, a few years ago he had given twenty thousand dollars for some much needed shelter renovations.

After Laura told him about the closing of the shelter, he let Laura know he wasn't happy about it. "I wish I had known this was going to happen—what a waste of my hard-earned money. If I wasn't already sick, this would have done me in. That twenty thousand dollars might just as well have been flushed down the toilet." He paused and settled down, resigned. "Oh, well, I guess there could have been far worse places to put my little stash. Live and learn."

Hank clutched Gracie's fur in his wrinkled left hand. She stayed beside him and looked up at him with affectionate approval of his massaging touch. Prone, enveloped in white sheets, and resting in the oversized hospital bed, Hank looked small and frail, but his opinions were still strong.

"Laura, the longer you live the more you realize that

there is a lot in life you just have to accept. That said, there are also times when you have to put your foot down. You know, Gandhi said something about animals that has stuck with me for a long time." He paused and thought back for a moment. "In fact, when Doc Pelot and I started the shelter back in the seventies, I wanted to make it our motto. You know, put it on a giant stone monument in front of the shelter where everyone could see it. I never got around to it. I guess I should have."

Laura leaned against the edge of the bed for support. "Do you remember what he said?"

"Sure. Well, at least the gist of it. He said that 'the greatness of a nation can be measured by the treatment of its animals.' I guess this makes me wonder about us. Do you agree with him?"

"Yes, Mr. Fisher, I know what he meant. I've heard the same message before, delivered in a different way." In fact, the Gandhi quote was one of her favorites. She looked down at the floor, not sure if she should say what was on her mind, but then she continued, " 'Inasmuch as ye have done it unto one of the least of these my brethren, ye have done it unto me.' "

Hank smiled. "That's right. That could go on our stone monument, too. You get it. It means we can't sit around and let this happen." Hank pushed a button on the side of his bed that elevated him to more of a sitting position. "Now, young lady, this is the kind of talk I like! So what are we going to do about it?"

"What can we do?"

"Plenty."

Todd put the last of the Christmas cookies Laura had brought him for lunch in the microwave. He liked to eat them warm. With his cookie supply depleted, he started on his afternoon duties. About twenty minutes into his routine, Todd got a call from George, who was asking for his permission to call an old acquaintance who worked at Paradise Valley Farms—the dairy that had advertised for help in the newspaper. Todd had told both his parents and Laura that was the best job he'd seen.

"Why do you want to call him?" Todd asked.

"Just to tell them that you've put in your application there and that you are a good worker, and to make sure they give you a good look. It doesn't hurt knowing people who can put in a good word for you."

"When will I start?"

"Todd, I'm not saying I can get you the job. I'm just saying I'll call over and see what's going on. What they're looking for. That kind of stuff."

"Okay, let me know."

Dealing with Todd's disability could try George's patience, but within a few minutes the frustrations had faded. He would smile, amazed at how Todd's mind operated, and a more pleasing and accepting attitude would prevail. He thought about calling Mary Ann and relaying the latest Toddism on the art of getting a job, but he decided to call Ed Lee instead. He searched through his old address book until he found the number. He had not talked to Ed in years and was not sure Ed would even remember him.

Until the early 1980s both Ed Lee and George had operated small dairy farms in different parts of Cherokee County. Big corporate dairies had driven them and most other small operators out of business. George's neighbor to the west, Hank Fisher, was the one notable exception. When he closed down his own operation, Ed had taken the *if you can't beat 'em join 'em* approach and got a job as a manager at Paradise Valley Farms. For his own part, George had moved from dairy farming to one of the dwindling areas where small-scale farming remained profitable—he primarily planted row crops such as wheat, soybeans, and corn, and had a few dozen head of beef cattle to keep him occupied in the winter months. He generated very modest profits from farming, but when that income was combined with his military disability pension—stemming from an injury to his leg during the Vietnam war—and Mary Ann's teacher salary, they got by.

Ed remembered George from random meetings of the old dairy farmers' cooperative and just from seeing him around town for the past sixty years. They spoke for a few minutes about the dairy business before George got to the point of the call. He tried to be as up front as possible about his son and his disabilities. "Todd is a hard worker," he said. "It just might take him a little longer to master some tasks. He'll do better when you show him how and don't just tell him how."

Ed didn't seem too worried. "With this position your son applied for, we're talking very manual work—power-washing the concrete floors, scrubbing the walls—stuff like that. Can he do it?"

"That would be easy for him, but his real passion is animals."

"George, I've got to tell you, we're a large corporate dairy. There is very little interaction with the cows. It's all very automated these days. Pretty amazing really. Not like the old days. You'd probably enjoy coming out and seeing us. There are computers everywhere."

"Hmm." George was not sure what to make of Ed Lee's observation. He decided it was up to Todd to figure it out. "Well, Todd is excited to work around animals. I guess that's a plus."

"Maybe, but he has to understand that our cattle are not like pets at an animal shelter; they are corporate investments. The cows are just like the human workers around here. They have to be productive or they get a pink slip."

George understood the point. "If you want to interview him, I'll talk to him about that and make sure he understands."

Ed thought a moment and then decided to take a risk. The job had been vacant for too long and needed filling. "George, I'd like to at least talk to Todd—you know, help him out if I can. Have him call me and we'll set up an interview. Of course, I can't promise anything beyond that."

At the top of Hayley's list of essentials for a properly run shelter was a commitment to impeccable cleanliness. All visitors found her shelter to be hospital clean and virtually odorless. Early on she explained to Todd that many people are so offended by animal waste that they will turn around and walk out at the first sign of a fouled cage. Not only did Todd and Hayley take each dog outside every few hours; whenever possible they also cleaned the cages twice daily to remove the inevitable accidents.

In the late afternoon, after Todd had called Laura and thanked her for bringing by his lunch and had cleaned the last cages, Doc Pelot arrived. He puffed on his pipe, causing it to billow smoke like an old steam engine. He joined Todd for their twice-weekly health check on every shelter pet. Halfway through, Hayley joined them. While they were walking down the aisles together, Hayley wanted to develop an agenda for their Friday staff meeting, but before she could bring up the subject, Doc Pelot looked around and asked, "How many critters do we have with us today?"

Hayley checked her inventory sheet. "We've been up and down this week. Today, we're at forty-eight."

Their capacity was fifty, so Doc Pelot frowned. "You mean we're practically full?"

Hayley shrugged. "I'm afraid so, but I've started to put the word out that we're no longer accepting any new guests. I'll run a notice in the paper, but not everyone will see it. I sure don't look forward to turning anyone away, but what choice do we have?" Hayley looked at the two men as if to say, Don't blame me!

The vet expanded on the problem. "The shame of it is that most locally funded animal shelters won't take strays from outside their own jurisdiction, so there will be nowhere else for the animals to go."

Having no experience with the task of closing a shelter, the three of them spun their wheels for the next half hour and made little progress in generating ideas for further development at Friday's meeting. Todd tried to support Hayley by suggesting that she turn to her strength. It was her routine for solving every other problem, so Todd assumed it made sense for this one, too. "Should we make a list?"

Doc Pelot liked the idea and tapped his cane twice on the concrete floor like the senior statesman that he was. "This task is too big for us to get our minds around. We need to break down the problem into smaller pieces and get better organized. I'm not too worried about getting the building ready for demolition. That's not our problem. Let's just focus on these dogs and cats."

Hayley started by establishing their time frame. "We have only twenty days until they close us down. In the next few days let's try to come up with some ideas for pushing adoption rates sky-high."

She pointed to the kennels. "Ricky, Curly, Dylan, Variable Rate, Sylvester, Freddy Mac, Ranger, Hulk, Bird Dog, and a few others have been hanging around here for a long time. We just might not be able to place every cat and dog on such short notice. I have been calling shelters throughout the region to see if I can find some backup spots. You know, just in case." She looked over at Todd to gauge his reaction, but he turned his back to her.

Doc Pelot concurred. "That's all we can do. As far as I'm concerned, we have no other choice. With such a large population, we are going to have to look to other shelters for help."

Todd remained quiet and started tapping at the side of a cage with his red Converse tennis shoes. Hayley recognized that he was pawing like an anxious horse. She knew why. Even at the risk of aggravating the old vet, she felt it was better to get everything out in the open. "What's wrong, Todd?"

He turned around to face Hayley and Doc Pelot. This was one of the few areas where the three of them disagreed. In the past they had tiptoed around the problem, but now it had to be addressed head-on. Todd rubbed his nose nervously and then began to pull on a tuft of light brown hair that jutted out just above his forehead. When he was ready, Todd quit fidgeting, stood tall, and spoke assertively. "I don't like that idea. I don't like our dogs and cats going to other shelters." He paused and took a deep breath. "These other places *kill* their animals."

Hayley, impressed with his acknowledgment of the reality, though saddened by his blunt reminder, sighed deeply and echoed his concern. "I don't like it either, but we don't always have a choice. This time more than ever."

Doc Pelot looked at both of them and tried to end the debate before it really got going. "Listen, however bad it is putting these dogs in kill shelters, it's better than asking me to put fifty dogs and cats down on some snowy afternoon because we haven't found a home for them. That's what the city has instructed me to do. Now, I'm not going to do it, so you two are going to have to figure out something else. But I say that if we're lucky enough to find a few shelters willing to help us out, we better not turn up our noses or turn down a helping hand. That's the way it has to be."

Todd felt cornered and didn't know what to do. Still, this option was unacceptable to him. "I'll find families for all of them."

"You're going to have to hurry. Less than three weeks and forty-eight dogs and cats needing homes? That's a very tall order." Frustrated, Doc Pelot shuffled off without saying another word. However much Todd, the young idealist, hoped for the best from the world, it would be Pelot, the old vet, who would be left to deal with a real-world mess.

After Mary Ann got home from Crossing Trails High School, she and George addressed invitations to their annual holiday party, always held on the last Sunday before Christmas. Given the fifty-year history of their event, George suggested to her that it would be easier to send out an announcement when they finally decided *not* to have the party. That would save them a great deal of work.

She rubbed his shoulders to show her gratitude. "Good try, George, but keep writing."

George brought up his call to Ed Lee.

"Do you think he's interested in Todd?" Mary Ann asked.

"I don't think he would have offered to interview him if there wasn't at least a chance. He said the industry has changed a lot in the last twenty years. He emphasized that it was a big business with lots of computers."

"That's obvious, George. What do you think he was really trying to say?"

"I'm not sure," he hedged, which was a whole lot easier to say than what he suspected Ed Lee meant. There were probably limited opportunities for Todd in a modern, high-tech dairy operation. Still, it was a job, a good place to start.

"When is Todd coming by?"

"Soon. I told him we would put an extra plate out for him and that you were making that tuna casserole he likes."

"I'll finish up dinner if you'll set the table."

"Deal."

About twenty minutes later Todd came through the back door, kissed his mom on the cheek, and asked, "So what's the big news Dad was talking about?"

She pointed to the living room. "Go find out."

Todd settled into a chair across from his father's recliner. Christmas sat beside him and Todd tucked his hand into the dog's collar.

George looked up from the paper. "Hello, gentlemen. How are you?"

"We're good."

Todd and Christmas both seemed to stare at George, eager for the scoop. George could tell that after spending the entire day at work with Todd, Christmas was glad to be home. The shelter was a high-energy place for an older dog. A spot by the fireplace suited him just fine. George wondered if it was time for Christmas to retire from his shelter duties with Todd and start taking it easier. He then realized that whether it was time or not, it was about to happen. George felt a little sad about the dog's advancing age. "You both look good to me, but maybe a little tired."

Hearing George's voice, Christmas wagged his tail and got up off the floor. George called the dog over to his side and gave his black fur a good rubdown. The dog appreciatively nuzzled George with his nose as if to say, Yes, George, I've missed you, and I will enjoy taking things a little easier.

Once satisfied that the old dog had been shown the proper respect, George turned his attention to his son. "The reason I asked you to stop by is that I've got good news. You've got an interview out at the dairy. Ed Lee, that old friend of mine I told you about, wants you to give him a call. Do you think you might like working with cows?"

Todd did not hesitate. "I like cows, but I like dogs better." Todd then pondered the details. "How much money do I make?"

George put his hand out like a traffic cop. "Whoa, Todd. Not so fast. I said you have an interview. Remember, that just means they'll talk to you. If they think you're a good fit, then they'll offer you a position and tell you the salary."

"I think I'm a good fit."

"We'll see. Most people think they're a good fit." George tried to go over the interviewing process with Todd and then, taking Ed Lee's advice to heart, cautioned Todd about the differences between a shelter and a dairy. "Todd, you need to understand that a corporate dairy is about making money with cows; a shelter isn't about making money with dogs. The dairy is a business."

"I like money."

George tried to make it clearer. "The shelter business is about keeping dogs and cats safe. The dairy business is about making milk. It's different." George was not sure how to explain it any better, but he tried once more. "In a dairy, the cows are like workers that stay for a long time, and in a shelter the dogs are like guests or friends that are staying overnight with you and then going to their new home."

Todd looked back down at Christmas for reassurance and said, "I've already been wondering about not having a job. I think I need to make it work even if a dairy is different from a shelter."

George assented. "I think you're right. This might be the best thing on the job menu." He handed Todd a piece of paper. "Here is his number. Tomorrow, call Ed Lee, set up an appointment time, and see what you think."

CHAPTER 9

ON THURSDAY afternoon, after Todd exercised the last dog, he took a break from his shelter duties to gas up his truck. While he was filling up he called Ed Lee and confirmed his interview time. He checked his messages and saw that Brenda had called again. Todd called her back. She had some ideas she needed to investigate further and wanted to know a good time when she might get back to him and Hayley, perhaps in a joint phone call. Todd switched to his calendar function and they agreed that the perfect time for her to call the shelter would be during Friday's staff meeting. Brenda gave Todd a hopeful hint: "I'm getting excited about this idea. I've just got to convince some people to help us out."

"You're the Problem Solver."

On Friday morning Laura and Todd crowded around Hayley's desk for their weekly staff meeting. This time the agenda was not about dog food or heartworm updates. They were trying desperately to formulate strategies to save their existing pet population and address the future needs of a county that would soon have no animal shelter. They had each committed to show up at the meeting with an idea or two. For his part, Todd told them that he had enlisted the Problem Solver, but they were going to have to wait awhile before they could talk to her. "She has to stay late working on the evening news, so I don't think she gets up this early."

Hayley floated her idea next. She suggested that they might donate their cages and other fixtures to another like-minded shelter. In exchange for giving them their equipment, they might ask to transfer four or five dogs and cats to the other facility. Hearing no objections, she agreed to make some inquiries.

Laura passed along the gist of her most recent discussion with Hank Fisher. "He told me that he was talking to his lawyer and the mayor to see if there are options for converting our shelter into a private not-for-profit corporation."

Doc Pelot was older, but his memory was vivid and crisp. "Hank and I talked about this idea of his years ago—before the county and the city took on the shelter partnership. It would require raising donations, which won't be easy these days."

Laura agreed. "That's right, but Hank thinks that someday Crossing Trails could have a scaled-back facility without the county's help. He told me to pass along that he is feeling much better. He hopes that over the coming days he will get his strength back and be able to pursue these ideas further. He also said"—Laura tried to mimic the old man's deep gruff voice—"Tell them to take good care of my dogs!"

"You tell him to worry about his own health, and that my dogs and cats are doing just fine." Doc Pelot lit his pipe and got back to his major worry. "I had an idea of my own. What if we contacted the chamber of commerce and got every member to sponsor one dog or cat? They could take one of our pets during the day and show him off, sending out e-mails to their customers. Again, it's a way to get our pets out into the limelight so they can strut their stuff."

The others were impressed by the old vet's marketing savvy. Hayley encouraged him to pursue it. "Sounds great. Can you do it?"

"Honey, I'm not too old to pick up the phone."

Todd checked his watch. "We need to call Brenda."

Hayley put her desk phone on speaker and dialed the number of the TV station.

After introductions were exchanged, Brenda got to her forte: problem solving. "I am so sorry to hear about the shelter, but I've been working on an idea that just might work. It's not an original idea, but I saw a story from one of our affiliates in Minnesota, and it occurred to me that we might be able to pull off something similar here. According to my research, only twenty percent of pets are acquired from shelters. . . ."

Hayley confirmed her research. "That's right. It's a problem for us. People convince themselves that they have to have a very specific breed of dog, so they go to breeders or they make an impulse purchase from a pet store."

"So, imagine this. . . . What if I could get you space in one of the busiest malls in the Midwest, for one afternoon only, to market your pets to thousands of shoppers?"

Laura bit. "That would beat the heck out of waiting for them to somehow come to us, but how could you do that?"

"To start with, I went to our news director and dug through hundreds of press releases. It wasn't hard to find one from the Mall of the Prairie. They would love for us to do a story on their Santa, their reindeer, and their giant tree. We won't though, because it's not that newsworthy. So I called Joan, the mall's publicity director, and shared with her an idea that just might make the Mall of the Prairie's holiday event newsworthy. The mall management might be able to make some prime space available for an afternoon at no charge. Of course, they're gambling that furry warm puppies and kittens might be an even better draw than an old man in a red suit."

Hayley was starting to see where this was going. "When is the event?"

"That's the hard part. It's on Sunday."

Laura's jaw dropped. "You mean this Sunday—in three days!"

"That's right. If you're interested, I'll let Joan know and she'll call you to make the arrangements."

Doc Pelot didn't care if they needed to be ready in three hours. "Tell her to call. We're in!"

"I can't do a story on just your shelter, but I can do something on all the shelters in the area and focus on your event at the mall as the backdrop. It'll get you a little attention."

"That's good! We'll take it." Todd looked at his fellow workers, hoping they too were pleased.

They broke up the meeting feeling a little less overwhelmed. Todd was relieved that everyone had liked Brenda's idea, but during the entire meeting he found his mind wandering to his date night with Laura. Before she left the shelter, Todd took her aside to discuss her choice of restaurant. "Do you think instead of Dutch food, we could have pizza?"

Laura laughed. "Todd, Dutch treat means we each pay for our own; it's not a kind of food."

As Todd got more comfortable in his relationship with Laura, he became less embarrassed by his miscues and took them in stride. He thought about it for a minute and said, "Oh, I didn't know that. Can we still do pizza?"

Laura hugged him gently. "Of course. Pepperoni?"

"I'll see you later."

❄

With their feet resting on a pet crate that was serving as a de facto coffee table in Todd's cabin, Laura and Todd finished off a large extra-cheese, extra-pepperoni pizza and an order of breadsticks. They leaned back, ready to burst, and Todd used the remote to start a dog-training video that had arrived the day before. The opening segment showed a professional trainer working with dogs and the human partners they were soon to be paired with. Each canine and human team was working together to perform a variety of tasks. The narrator explained, "The Heartland School for Dogs is a not-for-profit organization that provides guide, social, and service dogs to hundreds of deserving individuals in over thirty-four different states." The camera then cut to a shot of a dog helping a man in a wheelchair change his shirt. The dog grabbed the cuff of the sleeve in his mouth and gently pulled.

Todd had become a big fan of the Heartland School for Dogs and had made more than a few calls to Julie Bradshaw, the head trainer and expert dog handler featured in the videos. *Shy* was not a tag anyone ever tried to hang on Todd. When he hit a training plateau with Gracie, he would just pick up the phone and describe the problem to his new friend Julie, who seemed to enjoy helping him and hearing all about Gracie and Laura's unfolding partnership.

The more time she spent with Todd, the more Laura found herself being drawn to some of his clothing choices. She had taken to wearing black Converse tennis shoes. In contrast to her always crisp nursing uniforms, she was already inclined toward tattered and ripped blue jeans. For date night she decided to wear the Pet-a-thon T-shirt Todd had given her. He had received the shirt in exchange for a twenty-five-dollar donation. When she wore it the first time, he had commented, "You sure look a lot better in that than I would."

Resting on his haunches, with Todd's left arm draped around him, was Christmas—also alertly following the dog-training action on the screen. Striking a similar position, nested under Laura's right arm, was an equally enthralled Gracie. Class was in session. All four sets of eyes were mesmerized by the skills they were witnessing.

About fifteen minutes into the video, Todd was ready for a break. He paused the video and looked at the white retriever. He said her name in a firm way to signal that he was about to ask her to execute a command. "Gracie." After he was sure he had the dog's attention, he started a complex series of commands that had taken him two months of Friday afternoons to perfect. "Refrigerator!"

Even though he thought he was doing everything just like in the Heartland video, for the first month he had gotten nowhere. Todd had e-mailed Julie Bradshaw a video, and she could tell right away what he was doing wrong with Gracie.

"Todd, you can't combine that many steps," Julie had told him. "You have to break it down and teach her one step at a time. Each step has to be broken down further, too."

Gracie stood in front of the refrigerator waiting for the next command and Todd issued it: "Tug!"

There was an old towel tied to the handle of the

refrigerator door. Gracie grabbed it and pulled the door open. Tugging had started out being a game and then, slowly over a few weeks, Todd was able to move the tugging toy (a towel with knots in it) onto the object that he wanted her to open. Because of the suction, the door on the old refrigerator was difficult to open. In the beginning, he had had to open it for her and repeatedly praise her. Now she confidently gave it a sufficient yank on her own.

Todd issued the next command: "Dr Pepper." Gracie then reached in and gently removed a plastic bottle of soda, holding it near the top where the bottle was narrower. According to Julie, the ability to handle objects gently is one reason that retrievers often make such great service dogs. She told Todd, "Retrievers have very soft mouths. They can pick up a piece of paper without wrinkling it or even staining it with saliva."

"Close the door!" Todd commanded. Gracie positioned herself on the other side of the door and used her front paws to push the door closed. This move was also anything but easy to execute. Todd had had to break it down into several steps and make a game of jumping up on the wall and then expanding the jumping command to include cabinet doors, bathroom doors, kitchen drawers, and, ultimately, the refrigerator door.

"Fetch, Gracie!" Gracie brought the plastic bottle to Todd and gently released it to Todd's control. Todd profusely and excitedly praised Gracie and then fed her one of the small training treats.

Several months earlier, when Gracie had successfully completed "refrigerator retrieval," Todd had made a video of the whole process and e-mailed it to Julie. She had e-mailed him back: "A+ work to you and Gracie!"

Although they had never met in person, Julie and Todd enjoyed sharing dog-training stories. Julie was curious about Gracie and Laura's unfolding partnership, and Todd was more than willing to keep her posted. After a few exchanges of videos and e-mails, Julie knew that Todd had limitations, but at the same time it was obvious to her that he had an instinctive talent for dog training that could not be taught.

Todd printed out the e-mail from Julie Bradshaw and showed it to Laura. Although she was fully capable of getting her own soda, and rarely asked Gracie to do such things for her, she nonetheless appreciated Todd's carefully choreographed training exercise. She realized that for the wheelchair- or bed-bound individual, these skills were at the very core of what service dogs must learn to do.

Todd handed Laura her Dr Pepper and hit "Play" on the remote. Todd was impressed by Julie and her dogs and put words to what he expected his own dog must be feeling: "I know; you're good too, Christmas!" He then pulled the Lab closer. "You're fantastic."

Ten minutes later the Heartland School training video came to an end. Using the remote, Todd turned off the television and asked Laura, "Did you like it?"

"It was pretty good. The way Julie got the dog to pull the

wheelchair was excellent. I like how she pointed out that the tugging and retrieving moves are the foundation for so many routines. Watching her makes me appreciate what you've done with Gracie and what Gracie does for me."

Todd threw the pizza box in the trash. "Do you want some ice cream?"

"Are you kidding? I'm stuffed."

Todd hesitated, wondering if now was a good time to discuss an issue that was troubling him. He set his right hand next to Laura's left hand so that they barely touched. It was silent in the room for a few seconds before Todd said, "There is something I want to talk about."

Laura wasn't used to Todd framing a discussion so seriously. Usually he just dove in without a drum roll. She took her right hand away from Gracie and used it to push the hair from her face. "What?"

He looked at Laura and tried to gather his nerve. This was largely unexplored territory for Todd. He felt like he was blindfolded and walking on stepping-stones across a deep and dark lake. One misstep and he would go in, headfirst. At the same time, he trusted Laura. With her, the stones always seemed to be exactly where he needed them to be. Time and time again he had put his foot out, trusted, and found solid ground.

It was hard enough to say, so he didn't embellish it. "I get my words confused a lot. Some people call that a disability. "

The words were short, but the pain was long-standing. Although he had been told his whole life that he was disabled, he didn't often see himself in such terms. He squirmed about on the sofa, trying hard to find a comfortable position. His chin drooped slightly as he looked away from Laura and stared at the blank television screen, trying to keep his composure. He moved his hand slightly closer to hers—hoping she would not pull away and leave him stranded all alone with the unfortunate reality of his limitations.

Laura knew that Todd was trying desperately to be honest with her. She appreciated how vulnerable he was at that moment. She leaned in closer to him and rested her hand on top of his. Laura knew that she might very well have been the first person he had opened up to about this, his most sensitive of subjects. She wanted to respond carefully and to be just as honest. "I know, Todd. I'm disabled, too. We both are. That's okay."

It took all the courage he had left to finish the point. "I'm not smart, like you."

Laura knew this was hard for Todd, and she felt his pain stab at her own heart in a very palpable way, almost making it skip a beat. She sighed and squeezed his hand gently. "Todd, listen to me." She reached up and held his chin so he could not avert his eyes. "You're smart in all the ways you need to be smart."

Todd tried to probe deeper into the blurry realm of his disability. "I don't know if I'll ever make a lot of money or get another good job." He looked around his cabin and smiled. "Even with my mom helping me, I'm messy. That's part of my disability."

Laura leaned her forehead on Todd's shoulder and muttered, "Sometimes when I think people are watching me walk, I turn red and want to be invisible. I feel broken. Not whole. It's hard, isn't it?"

"Gracie, Christmas, and I think you're perfect."

She lifted her face to look up at Todd. "Thank you. You accept me the way I am, and, Todd, I accept you for who you are. You're the best person I know in the whole world." She squeezed his arm. "I don't care that you can't do calculus or recite Shakespeare. Lots of people can do that, but I don't know anybody who does what you can do with animals, and people, too. Every day you make my life a better place. You make the whole world a better place. No one can do that like you do."

Todd beamed and looked straight into her eyes. "Thank you."

"That's why you're my best friend."

"And you'll always be mine, Laura."

Todd felt reassured enough to reach his foot out again and hope that he would find a solid stone to support him on his journey across his deep lake of fear. "Laura, I have to make some decisions soon and I don't know what to do. Can you help me?"

"Of course. I'll try."

"I have an interview out at the dairy next week. I like

cows, but I'd rather work with dogs. I don't know that I want to work there."

Laura pulled him closer. "Todd, I'm so proud of the work you do at the shelter. You're good at it." She removed her hand from his and said with all the conviction she could muster, "If working with dogs is what you want to do, then, Todd, you must do it."

"But that would mean I may have to work at a shelter in a different town. Hayley and I are sending out our résumés all over."

She took his hand back. "I wouldn't like it if you moved."

"Me either. That's why I don't know what to do."

"People go off to other places or away to school all the time, and their friends . . . best friends . . . even their boyfriends and girlfriends—they all wait for them. They talk on the phone; they visit. We can do it."

Todd's eyes dropped. "I'm not sure I can move. It's not just you. My parents would hate it. I might, too. With my disabilities, maybe I need help sometimes. The only place I have ever lived is on this farm. I don't know anything else."

She held him closely. "I guess that leaving home would be scary. I understand that." Laura looked up and saw that the sun was setting. She checked her watch. It was nearly 5:30. She had promised her parents she would be home by six so that she would not be driving on country roads after dark. "It's getting late. We can talk more tomorrow."

"Do you have to go?"

"Yes. I better."

Todd stood up and offered Laura his hand.

"What! That's Gracie's job. I don't know if it's the right thing, but I'll let you in on a secret. Even when I don't need the help, when my arthritis is in remission, like today, I still let her help me. Gracie just loves to serve—to help—so I never deny her the opportunity." She kissed Gracie lightly right between her affectionate eyes before giving the white retriever the first in a series of commands. "Stand." Once Gracie was up, she gave the next order: "Stay."

Todd had taught her to be very firm when giving this second command. Gracie had to know that if she balked, Laura could fall and hurt herself. When Gracie was stable, Laura completed the last part of the command, "Brace," and she rose out of the chair. "Good girl!" Once up, she held her arms open wide, inviting a hug from Todd.

Todd stepped into her arms and said, "I wish you didn't have to go."

"I'd like to be able to stay. Don't worry, Todd, we can work this out. We have time. I'm excited for Sunday." She mimicked the baritone voice from Channel Six: "The Problem Solver!"

Todd allowed their embrace to linger longer than he ever had before. He could feel his heart leaping in his chest. He kissed her lightly on the cheek and said, "Thanks for coming out and watching Julie Bradshaw with me."

She blushed a little and smiled, then bent down and patted Christmas. "I'll see you both on Sunday." Gracie wagged her tail and walked by Laura's side to the door.

Christmas paced about anxiously, as if not at all happy about the departure of his two friends.

Todd walked alongside Laura and Gracie to the car and made sure Laura got safely out onto the road that led back to town. The sound of her car leaving the driveway seemed to hang in the air like the rumble of distant thunder. Once back inside his cabin, Todd sat on the sofa with Christmas for a very long time trying to make sense of his rapidly shifting life. The sun slipped slowly behind McCray's Hill, and the room became dark, but still he did not move. What Laura had said to him was nice. He appreciated it, but he still wasn't convinced she understood. His heart felt heavy and ached. He did not like the feeling. He could not imagine a world where he had to go months without being with Laura. Nor could he imagine a world where he did not work with dogs. Something was seriously wrong with his having to choose one or the other. Todd pulled Christmas closer to him so he could fill up the empty space that Laura had left behind.

As was their habit near bedtime, his parents called to make sure Todd didn't need anything. Once he assured them that he was fine, he got up off the sofa, put on his hat and coat, and walked outside with Christmas. The air was cold and damp, and the wind blew gently from the north. The sky was clear, and he could see the dense band of stars that his father called the Milky Way.

All the things he wanted—a good job, independence, more time with Laura—they all seemed far away like the

stars. When he was convinced Christmas had had sufficient time to finish his outdoor business, he let out a sharp
whistle. Christmas joined him and they both went back
inside and got ready for bed. Once in his flannel pajamas,
Todd picked up the dog-training DVD and put it back in its
case. He decided to visit Heartland's Web page. He'd seen
some T-shirts he liked in their Web store and decided they
might make nice Christmas gifts. After he ordered one for
Laura and a slew of smalls for his numerous nieces and
nephews, he decided to type a quick note to Julie. He navigated to the Contact Us page of their site and typed in the
little comment box.

> Julie,
> Just watched that training video you told
> me about. You were great. I've got bad news.
> They're closing the shelter in Crossing Trails. I
> need to get a new job. Do you know anyone who
> is looking for an assistant shelter manager?
> Thanks,
> Todd.

After making sure there were no red warnings from
his best friend the spell-checker, Todd located his résumé
from his saved documents, attached it to the e-mail, and hit
the Send button.

Once he was situated in bed for the night, Todd turned
off the lamp, closed his eyes, and said a prayer, asking that

Sunday's event would go well, better than planned, that Laura and his family would stay safe, and that more dogs would find homes. Most of all, he prayed that all the things in life that did not make sense might finally make sense.

He rolled on his side and extended his arms around Christmas. The black dog felt good. He could smell the fresh night air still clinging to the dog's coat. Christmas exhaled heavily and gave out a snug little whimper of gratitude. His tail swept back and forth twice and then all was quiet inside Thorne's cabin.

CHAPTER 10

EARLY SATURDAY morning, George was leaning against the corral fence that flanked the north end of their old red barn, and he was feeling the wind move across his face. He read its message: cold and brisk. Even with the first snow falling days earlier, he had been slow this year to accept the arrival of winter. That morning he had swapped his regular jeans for the flannel-lined ones that waited for him on the top shelf of his closet like a trusted friend, another year older. It was a comforting treat, feeling the warm cotton around him.

George had been up for a long time. He had done the milking chores for Hank at dawn and then returned home to do his own work. George's conversation with Ed Lee had made him realize what a dinosaur he was when it came to milking. Hank was even worse. His equipment was antiquated. He and Hank had worked in the business long before the advent of modernization, globalization, corporatization, and a long list of other "izations" that had put an end to most family dairy farms. At the time, George had been pleased to let the business go. It's hard to pour your sweat and soul into a financial enterprise when you can do little more than break even. More than that, it's hard to make an effort at something that others don't seem to value. For all these reasons, it surprised him that he was so enjoying his brief return to dairy farming. Helping Hank brought back a lot of fond memories, although he wondered if time was causing him to romanticize the whole business just a little.

An impulse swept over him and he went inside the red wooden barn, built just after the turn of the last century by his great-grandfather, and walked to a dusty and dark corner where he had not ventured for a very long time.

George tried to shake an old pain out of his right leg as he made his way to the far end of a cluttered aisle. He flipped on a light and surveyed the old milking equipment, machinery, tools, and boxes that were still stored beneath tarps and on pallets to stay dry and protected. Many of the things that represented George's past were seemingly waiting for him, suspended in time.

It was a painful realization that Hank and his fading dairy operation were, in a lot of ways, like this old equipment—something treasured and valued before but now obsolete. With his poor health, there was no way Hank could continue in the business without finally hiring some help. George knew that Hank—no matter how much money he had—would never spend it on hired help or anything else that might make his life easier. Soon Hank would sell his small herd and that would be the end of it.

George lifted one of the tarps and surveyed more of the old dairy equipment. It had been a long time since he had rummaged through these memories. The 1960s—and then the '70s, the '80s, the '90s, and the first decade of the new millennium—had slipped by so quickly. He remembered the cold winter mornings when he had milked with his father and grandfather, his treasured boyhood dog, Tucker, and the hours the two of them had spent exploring the banks of neighboring Kill Creek.

It all seemed so far away, not just in time, but also in other ways not so easily measured. Everything had been different then; harder yet more real. He wondered if he was becoming a typical old codger, convinced that the good times were gone forever. It also occurred to him that perhaps he was right. Something significant had been lost from their lives, and his reaction to that loss was entirely appropriate.

He continued his search under the tarps until he found an old steamer trunk. He couldn't even remember exactly what was in it. The keys to the trunk were attached to the lock with a little piece of chicken wire. He opened the lock and cautiously lifted the dusty lid.

The contents were more dumped inside than organized in any systematic way. He found papers, owner's manuals to tools and equipment—most of which had long ago been discarded—some old clothing, and a few old black-and-white photographs. He wasn't in the mood to dig deeper through the contents. Just as he was shutting the trunk lid the overhead light glimmered on a small piece of wood trim and glass. He hesitated and then dug down and removed a framed photo. He pulled it out for a closer look. He had forgotten about this picture.

It was of him as a small boy riding on his grandfather's tall shoulders. Bo McCray was carrying a large and heavy milk can with his right arm while clutching one of George's tiny legs with the other. George blew the dust off the framed photo. It was still dirty, so he removed a cloth handkerchief from the back pocket of his jeans and wiped the picture clean. He wondered if Mary Ann had ever seen this.

Naturally, after his nostalgic voyage through the barn, George wondered if Todd's working in the dairy business was somehow preordained, almost inevitable. The more he thought about it, the more logical it seemed. Todd's working at the dairy would tie up all the loose ends in his son's life and their family history. This old photograph said so much. He wanted to share it with Todd and try to explain to him that he had the chance to become a fourth-generation Kansas dairy farmer. To George, that meant continuity with the land and the place he called home.

George left the barn and headed back to the house, pocketing his new treasure in his jacket. He poked his head through the back door and found Mary Ann at the sink, washing dishes. "I'm going down to see Todd. Do you want to go?" he asked.

"I can't right now, but why don't you take Christmas with you? He could use the exercise." As he was prone to do, the Lab had wandered up from Thorne's cabin to their house early that morning. He had scratched on the back door until Mary Ann let him inside.

"Come on, Christmas! Let's go see Todd." George and Christmas walked down the east side of the hill to the cabin, George all the while tossing a tennis ball he kept in his jacket pocket, handy for Christmas. George's leg still felt stiff and sore, but the muscle ache loosened with light exercise, and by the time he made it halfway down the hill he was moving well. Christmas seemed to have a similar experience. After a few minutes he was eager to chase after the tennis ball and enjoy a brisk morning romp.

George waited patiently for Christmas to amble back with his prize. In the distance George could see his small herd of Angus cattle moving slowly up from the creek. "Come on, Christmas! Bring me the ball."

The morning light poked through a small hole in an otherwise overcast sky, and what almost appeared like a giant spotlight fell on the field where the dog was trotting. George held his hand up to shade his eyes from the sun's sudden glare. Old as he was, Christmas still moved gracefully. George loved to watch the dog's elegant motion.

When Christmas caught up, George took the tennis

ball and they made their way down to the bottom of the hill and to the front door of Thorne's cabin.

"Good morning, Dad." Todd was glad to see George, but he also seemed preoccupied. "I have to be at the shelter by twelve. I'm meeting lots of people. We're getting ready for tomorrow."

"Don't worry, Todd, I won't stay all day." George took a seat on the sofa while Christmas greeted Todd as if it had been weeks and not hours since he had last seen him.

"Dad?" Todd turned away from the dog and looked at George. "How do you decide if something is a good Christmas present?"

George wondered where this conversation was going, but decided it was best just to go along for the ride and enjoy it. "If the person likes the gift, then it's a good gift." George looked at his son affectionately and shared with him an observation that he and Mary Ann had made on many occasions. "You're an excellent gift giver."

"I try to give people things they need."

George pointed to the black Lab resting on the floor of the cabin. "That was a good gift."

Todd sank down beside the dog. "I agree."

"What would you like this year?" George asked his son.

"I think I would like to stop worrying all the time. About work, friendships, where to live . . . stuff like that." Todd paused. "Sometimes I feel like I don't know where I belong."

This statement bothered George. "Todd, I hope you

know you'll always belong here with your mom and me. This is your home just like it's ours."

"Dad, can I ask you something else?" Todd looked at his father and gave voice to something he had been thinking about for days, probably for weeks—maybe even months. "What does it feel like to be in love?"

As prepared for Todd's bluntness as George usually was, the question surprised him. He wondered if this was what was lingering behind Todd's concern about where he belonged. Here was an area of discussion that the two of them had never explored. George felt a little uneasy. He tried to remember how it had felt for him when he was a young man and experiencing romantic love for the first time.

"I guess it feels pretty scary at first. When you get it right, it's very nice. When you get it wrong, it can really hurt."

Todd's face lit up, like he knew exactly what his father was talking about. "How do you make sure you get it right?"

Todd deserved to know the adult answer, but it was a hard truth. George put his hand on his son's shoulder and did his best to answer. "Most of us spend our lives trying to get love right. We go through periods when nothing could be easier than being in love, and then there are times when getting it right seems almost impossible. We make mistakes. I did. You will, too. The main thing to remember is that it's always worth the effort—trying to get it right."

Todd put his hand on Christmas. Love seemed to trickle up from the dog's black fur. "With dogs, getting love right is easy."

"Getting love right will be easier for you than it is for the rest of us. Just like being a good gift giver, when it comes to the love department, you're a natural." George helped Todd get where he suspected his son was headed. "Are you asking me this because of Laura?"

"Yes—maybe I'm in love with Laura."

George tightened his grip on his son's shoulder. It was his turn to feel protective toward Todd and to worry about the inevitable heartbreaks of romantic love. He had to admit he felt a little anxious about confronting another milestone of his son's development. George loosened his grip and said, "Love is like the prairie grass in the meadow behind this cabin—if you give it time, deep roots will take hold. Once that happens, it's nearly impossible to dig it up, and it will grow strong and spread till it chokes out all the weeds. So take your time with this, Todd. Don't rush it. Let the roots of your love grow strong."

Todd thought another moment and then asked, "Did Mom still love you while you were gone in the war?"

"That she did. There's a whole box of letters up in the closet to prove it. She wrote me every day."

Todd looked at his cell phone and George could tell that Todd was about to shut down. It had been a good conversation. There was no need to push it any further.

Then George remembered the reason for his visit.

"I want to show you something," he said, taking the old framed photo out of his pocket and handing it to Todd.

Todd studied it for a few minutes. "Who is that man?"

"That's your great-grandfather, Bo McCray. You would have really liked him."

Todd continued to look at the picture more closely. "I know who he was—Grandpa Bo. But I never got to meet him. Who's the little boy?"

"It's me, Todd."

"That's you!" Todd exclaimed in the astonished way only Todd could.

"Yep. We were coming up from the barn. Just finished the milking. I was hitching a ride on his shoulders. He liked to carry me that way. I always felt I was riding on the back of a giant."

"Grandpa Bo sure looks happy. I think he liked having you on his shoulders."

George missed his grandfather, and he felt a moment of heavy loss. He looked away, afraid that a tear might appear. He exhaled long and slow and then looked at his son. "I suppose he did. He was pretty good about loving dogs and people—just like you. You two are a lot alike."

George let another minute or two of silence set in. It had been a privilege to ride on the shoulders of Bo McCray. He wondered if he could ever be such a figure for his own son.

Todd looked at the grainy black-and-white photograph. "It looks like a long time ago."

"It was. Sometimes it seems farther away than I can imagine." George remembered the reason for the trip down the hill. "Todd, I just want you to know that you did great finding something decent on the job menu and jumping out there and trying to get it." He stopped just short of telling Todd that he wanted him to go into the dairy business. Like Bo, and like George, Todd would make his own way in the world. "I thought you might like to have the picture to put on your wall."

"Thank you, Dad. I think you're a good gift giver. I like the picture."

George stood up. "Your mom and I are planning on driving to the mall on Sunday. Let us know if anything changes."

WHEN THE McCray family arrived at the shelter on Sunday, the *Channel Six News* truck was already in the lot. Brenda Williams had asked her crew to drive out to Crossing Trails to get some shots of the dogs and cats in their cages and of the volunteers loading them up for the trip. The crew complained about driving for two hours to get fifteen seconds of footage, but Brenda was in charge, insisting that before-and-after shots would be powerful. "We can open with the shelter shots and then show pets with their new owners, after the adoptions take place. And wait until you meet the shelter director." Still they grumbled. But once they went inside the shelter, saw the dogs and cats, and met Hayley, they decided the Problem Solver, once again, was spot-on.

Hayley was nervous about their kickoff event. An hour earlier she had finished one of a series of exhaustive meetings with the mayor and the city manager to work out the details of closing the shelter. The city manager confirmed the year-end date for vacating the building. Each little step taken made the unimaginable seem painfully real. The shelter was really going to close. The mayor tried to soften the blow. "You know, Hayley, even if the county had not pulled out of the shelter partnership, we were going to have to make changes. Every city department has had to cut its budget so we can keep our expenses in line with our revenues. Things were going to be tough either way."

Haley shook her head. "Is that supposed to make me feel better, Mayor?"

Arriving at the shelter later, Todd called out, "Hayley? I'm here. Are you ready to go?"

She'd been there since 6:45 that morning, grooming and feeding dogs, gathering supplies, cleaning out cages, and double- and triple-checking her master "to-do" list for their event. Hayley and Todd had selected the fifteen most adoptable dogs for the event, as well as two cats. Hayley made an effort to get each of them taken outside for one last potty break before setting off on the long drive to Kansas City for the day's event.

"Ready as I'll ever be, Todd." Hayley ran down her list one last time and let out a deep breath. "Let's go."

As all the shelter volunteers, among them George, Mary Ann, and Laura, gathered in the lobby, Hayley and Todd handed out directions to the Mall of the Prairie and reviewed the plans for how they would set up once they arrived.

Laura slipped her arm around Todd's shoulder and gave him a friendly squeeze. "This is going to be fun!"

He squeezed back. "It's not just fun, Laura. It's work!"

"Work that you love doing, Todd."

George took note of what she'd said and exchanged a look with Mary Ann.

Hayley wrapped a red and green scarf around her neck as she rallied her troops. "Let's load up and get on the road!"

Less than two hours later the shelter caravan converged in a parking lot at the Mall of the Prairie, just as great big white snowflakes began falling from the sky. The mall had been built in the 1980s and was located in an affluent neighborhood. Although the place was slightly dated, its interior was well maintained, with polished tile floors, lush green plantings, fountains, and public seating areas. Besides large, upscale stores like Macy's and Saks, there were smaller shops, as well as a busy food court and plenty of kiosks that sold everything from calendars to cell phones to roasted chestnuts. Because it was one of the last shopping weekends before Christmas, the place was packed. Part-time mall security officers were assisting with the parking, and traffic was backed up all the way to the interstate.

The guys from the news truck set up the TV cameras inside the mall while Todd and the others unloaded the pets outside in a zone that had been set aside for them. When mall security arrived, they led the entire group of ten humans, fifteen dogs, and two cats to their assigned mall space. A few months earlier the area had housed a boutique filled with high-end designer clothing; now it was showcasing a far more valuable inventory.

Brenda had gone above and beyond her commitment to help get the space ready. She had taken photographs of the shelter animals, enlarged them to poster size, and plastered them on the former shop's plate-glass windows. The boutique was strategically located in one of the busiest wings of the Mall of the Prairie, and the posters were attracting considerable interest from passing shoppers, who watched with curiosity through the locked front doors as volunteers arranged crates for the cats and some temporary pens for the dogs.

By noon a small crowd of holiday shoppers was converging in front of the space, eager to see what was attracting the attention of the *Channel Six News* cameras. The cameramen encouraged them to hang around and find out.

Five minutes before their scheduled opening, Todd grabbed the leashes that were attached to the little Tibetan Terrier, Westin, and the pit bull–Lab mix, Earl, and he walked them both into a small fenced-in space the volunteers had assembled, complete with its own little gate, onto a red circular rug that Brenda had provided as the place where they planned to "show" the dogs. Taking out the note card Hayley had given him, he tested his lines in the microphone they'd set up. "Two great dogs. All adoption fees waived today."

Hayley decided that was not enough. "When the people come in, show them some tricks. We need something else," she said nervously.

"Hayley, I almost forgot!" Laura exclaimed.

When Laura's mother had ordered a new guide harness for Gracie she could not help herself and also ordered two dog vests that said ADOPT ME on one side, with the phone number for the shelter on the other. Laura pulled them out of her tote bag and handed them to Hayley, who took one look and said, "Perfect! Just what we needed." She rushed over and put them on Earl and Westin. Now they looked show ready.

At the appointed time, Brenda Williams, a familiar face to many shoppers, flung open the doors and welcomed the shoppers. "Come on in and see some really special dogs and cats!" Two dozen children and their parents gathered instantly around the fenced-in area where Hayley stood.

Todd handed Earl's leash to Mary Ann and stepped through the gate and onto the red carpet with Westin following close behind. The terrier had fully recovered from his infection and seemed very pleased to prance about and be the center of attention. When he was near the microphone, Todd commanded, "Sit!" The dog politely took a seat and looked up at Todd. He reached into his pocket and gave the dog a small reward. "Down, Westin." The dog immediately went down.

Todd then addressed the gathering crowd through the mic. "Westin needs a home. He can do a lot of wonderful things for you. Would you like to see?"

"Yes!"

Todd ran Westin through a series of exercises they had practiced many times—fetching, sitting, begging, barking, tugging, kissing, and rolling over—all to the crowd's pleasure and general amazement. "He's so cute!" a dozen people seemed to say at once.

Someone yelled out, "How much is he?"

Hayley stepped up to the mic and said, "He'll cost you lots of love, but no money. We're waiving all adoption fees. Our shelter is being closed, and we have to find these guys new places to live."

Mary Ann slipped her fingers into George's hand and squeezed as hard as she could. When she had George's attention, she threw a glance at Todd. "Your son is pretty awesome."

When Todd finished with Westin, he handed the dog's leash to Hayley, who walked the terrier closer along the edge of the crowd. She saw several adults copying down the shelter phone number. She returned to the microphone. "If you're interested in Westin, you can fill out the adoption paperwork at the table behind me." Westin lasted less than a minute before someone cried out, "I'll take him!"

Next Todd introduced the crowd to Earl, who had his own unique repertoire. Earl's patented reverse-spin move garnered the largest audience response, particularly among the children. After Todd worked with each dog, he gave the leash to one of his volunteer handlers, who walked the dog out into the audience and eventually out and around the mall. Each shopper was greeted with an affectionate tail wag and a warm set of longing eyes.

By three-thirty the shelter crew was really warmed up. It was then that they realized they had made one very terrible mistake. It was every merchant's nightmare. They had failed to bring along sufficient inventory and had to close up shop early. Earl, Westin, and all their pals would have a new Christmas home that year. Within a few days, these fine creatures would be perfecting their own magic trick. Todd did not have to teach them this one. With great stealth and cunning, each animal would steal away with its new family's heart.

That night, the *Channel Six News* featured the Mall of the Prairie and all the fun the shoppers were having visiting Santa and his reindeer, riding the holiday carousel, and checking out some unusually furry inventory. The Problem Solver urged her viewers to visit their local animal shelter and help some displaced dogs and cats find a home.

Her piece brought about a flurry of phone calls and visits to shelters over the next few days. For at least a while, demand was up and supply was down.

❄

While the other shelter workers were bringing pet adoption to the big city, Doc Pelot kept busy at home making sure the small town of Crossing Trails did what it could. He sat at his desk and pitched dogs to each member of the local chamber of commerce. By the end of the day on Monday, the shelter was turning into a ghost town of empty cages. All the cats were gone, and there were only twelve dogs left. All the hard work was beginning to pay off.

CHAPTER 12

MONDAY AFTER work Todd stopped in to see his parents on his way home. George and Mary Ann wanted to be sure he was prepared for his big interview at the dairy scheduled for Tuesday morning.

George tried to reinforce for Todd what he had said earlier, that the dairy was a business, and Mary Ann reminded Todd to dress neatly. "Being nicely dressed is a great way to show that you care and really want the job," she said. "This is not the time to be sloppy." To emphasize her point she teasingly pulled at his T-shirt, adorned with a full day's worth of pet dander, and kicked at his red Converse tennis shoes, stained by six months of swabbing the shelter deck.

"Should I wear my suit?"

Mary Ann thought about it and decided a suit would be too much. Besides, the one he had fit him poorly. "We bought that for your graduation, and you've filled out quite a bit since then. It doesn't fit you anymore. Just wear those nice blue dress pants and the green sweater you wore at Thanksgiving."

George playfully put Todd in a headlock. "In two weeks, you'll be wearing Brooks Brothers suits and running that dairy. Old Ed Lee will be looking for a new job."

Todd laughed and landed a fake uppercut to George's midsection.

"Nice one, Todd," George said, releasing his grip and brushing enough copper-colored dog hair off his son to weave a good-sized area rug. "Good luck tomorrow. You'll do great."

Later that night Laura and Gracie were making their last rounds at the Wellness Center. She enjoyed spending the end of her shift chatting with Hank about Todd, the dairy business, and, of course, the shelter. That night Hank was already asleep when she arrived. Laura sat in the side chair for a few minutes. She tried to send Hank her strongest and most healing sentiments. She pictured him in a clear healing light.

Gracie whined and her white tail wagged, breaking Laura's concentration. The dog seemed to be pleading. "What's wrong, girl?" Laura asked.

The dog seemed agitated, like she wanted to be released from her position. Laura gave the "good girl" signal she used to release Gracie from the stay or neutral position where she was trained to stay when she was working. The dog eagerly went to Hank's bedside and sat down, her bushy white tail still wagging. She whined and pawed at the bed frame repeatedly. Laura noticed that Gracie's tail wag was entirely different. It reminded her of the much slower and more purposeful movement of a large cat, like a tiger or a leopard.

"Gracie, Hank is sleeping, but don't worry, we'll come see him tomorrow." The dog persisted, and Laura was afraid she was going to bother Hank. "Gracie, quit it, get back over here."

The dog continued to whine, so Laura pushed herself out of the chair—a task that was a little more difficult without Gracie's help. Once on her feet, Laura moved bedside. Although the monitors that were strapped to Hank did not register a problem, Laura thought his breathing seemed forced, so she tried to wake him, "Hank, are you okay?"

He didn't respond.

Laura gave him a firm push. He finally opened his eyes and looked at her. But he seemed unfocused and quickly closed his eyes again. Laura pushed the emergency help button on the side of the bed and the Crossing Trails Wellness Center lost its sleepy demeanor.

The RN and Dr. Wilson, the physician on call, worked on the left side of the bed checking Hank's vital signs. Laura and Gracie remained on the right side, Laura clutching Hank's hand in her own, hoping that any minute the doctor would tell her not to worry, that everything was fine. She kept glancing up at him, but those words were not said.

CHAPTER 13

ED LEE rested his elbows on his cluttered desk, leaned toward the speakerphone, and said, "Send him in."

Todd completed his office interview with Ed in less than five minutes. The dairy manager could not help but be impressed: Todd was a healthy, strong, polite young man. Ed suspected that Todd would be a hard worker. On top of that, he had grown up on a dairy farm and came from a good family. Still, the work was hard—certainly not for everyone. Ed wasn't sure if Todd, for all his enthusiasm, had grasped the nature of the business.

"Would you like to take a tour of the dairy?"

Todd nodded, and Ed stood and pulled his walkie-talkie from his belt.

"Paul, this is Ed. I have the young man I told you about, Todd McCray, up in my office. He's ready for a brief tour."

"Ten-four," came a crackling voice in response. "I'll meet you at the work door."

"Paul will show you around. He would be your direct supervisor. Let's go down to the dairy barns and I'll introduce you."

Ed and Todd walked through the remainder of the dairy's office space, through the sections for accounting and marketing, and toward the exit that led to the barns. Although Todd wasn't exactly neat, he couldn't help but notice stacks of papers and dirty coffee cups everywhere in the office, mini-blinds caked with dust, and a broken computer heaped in a corner by the photocopier. A wall calendar by the drinking fountain indicated that it was May. His mother, who was constantly trying to tidy up his cabin, would not have approved.

Paul Vernon, a heavyset man with thinning red hair, pushed through one of the steel side doors and walked across the concrete floor to meet Ed and Todd. Paul shook Todd's hand. "Why don't you go through that door and take a look around outside the barns?" He pointed to the door. "I'll join you in a minute."

After Todd had walked out the door, Paul asked Ed, using the voice ten-year-old boys reserve to mimic the severely retarded, "Duhh, Duhh, Rrr . . . uuu . . . going . . . to . . . geeb . . . him . . . a . . . jaab?"

Ed wasn't amused. "Don't be a jerk, Paul. I've been telling you for two weeks to get someone in there to clean. I ran the ad for you, and you've not bothered to get anyone in here. The barns look awful. If the USDA makes one of their surprise inspections, they're going to write you up. You haven't gotten around to interviewing anyone, so I'm trying to help you out. What's the problem?"

Paul rolled his eyes at what he had already concluded was a bit of misguided do-gooding by Ed. "I want someone that'll do lots of work and very little talking. Can your kid handle it?"

"We'll see."

Paul walked out the back door and caught up with Todd, still not that happy about his newest responsibility. The Federal Department of Immigration and Naturalization did not have a field office anywhere near Crossing Trails, Kansas. Not so coincidentally, Paul Vernon had become lax on his paperwork. Much of the dairy's labor force consisted of migrants from Mexico who spoke little English, would do what they were told, and never complained. Paul's labor cost per gallon of milk produced was getting him high marks from headquarters. He was hoping for a nice bonus this year. Ed Lee was supposed to run the office and Paul was supposed to run the barns. Paul didn't like Ed's encroaching into his space. He didn't like someone else picking the people he had to supervise. Still, maybe the kid would work out.

Paul hurried Todd through the barns, making cursory comments about the automated feeders, the automated washers, the automated milking apparatus, and the seemingly automated cows, each confined to a small space for the remainder of her short life. He pointed to the thick red commercial hoses that were attached to the walls. "Those will be your best friends. They're high-pressure hoses. We use them to wash the cow crap off the floor."

While Paul focused on the equipment, Todd's attention kept reverting to the cows. Milk cows have large udders, but the hormones these cattle were given had caused elephantine, gross swelling. Several cows, even from a distance, seemed ill to Todd. Not only did the cows look unhealthy, but the barn was a mess. The valuable inventory of Paradise Valley Farms was stacked into stalls as tightly and neatly as two-liter bottles of soda pop in a grocery aisle, and they were standing ankle-deep in their own waste.

Todd felt the need to get right to work cleaning the pens. "Looks like you can use my help now. The pens are pretty dirty."

Paul had to admit that Todd was showing some initiative, so he tried to lighten up his attitude. "I guess that's why Ed Lee is hot to trot to get you hired. I had a few folks quit on me. They took their paychecks and went straight to Juárez. They never came back like they said they would."

Paul hurried Todd through the rest of the barns and back to Ed Lee's office. As Paul turned to leave, Ed helped Todd to a chair and said, "Just a second, Todd. I'll be right back."

He shut the door behind him and spoke briefly with Paul. "What did you think?"

"I guess he'll do. It's your call."

Ed wasn't sure what to do. He didn't particularly like Paul, but headquarters did, so he put up with him and tried to defer to him when he could.

Ed rejoined Todd. "What did you think?"

"The barns need cleaning, but I know how to do that."

"Todd, thanks for coming in. We have a few more interviews set up for this afternoon, but we should be able to make a decision in a few days. We'll call you one way or the other."

Ed walked Todd out to the parking lot. "Do you have big Christmas plans?"

"No. My brothers and sister usually drive out and my mom cooks a big dinner. Turkey."

"Sounds good."

Todd got in his truck, let the engine idle for a minute, and tried to ponder what had just happened. He had never seen or experienced anything like this before. The environment and atmosphere at the dairy were very different from those of the shelter. For reasons he could not explain, the dairy frightened him. He wished that Christmas could have been there with him. He missed the security the dog provided. He guessed this was what his dad had meant when he said the dairy was about making money and the shelter was about caring for animals.

Todd fastened his seat belt and pulled up to the security gate. He returned his visitor's pass to the guard. The guard took the plastic laminated card from Todd and said, "Thank you for visiting Paradise Valley Farms. Drive safely."

Todd nodded and drove off the lot to Buckley, a small town between Crossing Trails and the dairy, and got gas. While the tank was filling he read a text message from Hayley, "How did it go???"

Todd called her and explained, "Mr. Lee seemed nice, and I liked the cows. They need my help. The pens really need cleaning. The man who runs the barns is named Paul, and he is nothing like you. I don't think he would make a good shelter manager, but maybe dairies are different because they're more about money. Mr. Lee said he would think about it and give me a call. It pays more than the shelter, a lot more. I didn't ask, but he told me anyway."

"You seem a little uncertain. Do you want this one?"

Todd thought for a minute. He knew he needed to work, to make money, to have some purpose in life. He certainly didn't want to find himself moving back in with his parents, and he didn't like the idea that he might not have anything to do all day. He didn't want to move backward; he wanted to move forward—to be more independent, not less. Most important, he didn't want Laura to think he was irresponsible. If he didn't have a job, his future with Laura might be very limited. Still, the dairy didn't feel quite right to him. "I don't know if I want it, but I guess I need it. It's probably what's best."

CHAPTER 14

THREE DAYS after they had so successfully kicked off their holiday fostering event, Todd was digging through an old box of clothing that his mother had saved for him from various Halloweens and other holidays. He was trying to figure out exactly what to wear for his caroling date with Laura and her parents. Laura's mother was so proud of the doggie vests she had bought for the shelter that she had suggested that Todd and Laura should add two special features to the evening's event. "Why not bring a couple of shelter dogs along and maybe someone will see them and adopt one of them on the spot?"

Laura was not certain it was a great idea, but after discussing it with Todd and Hayley, they all decided that it was consistent with their strategy of getting the dogs out of the shelter and into the community. Hayley encouraged them. "Give it a try."

Laura conceded, "I guess you're right; we can try it and see what happens."

❄

At the bottom of the box Todd found the stocking cap with the protruding reindeer antlers he'd gotten as a gift from his brother Jonathan several years ago. He took the hat out of the box and tried it on to see if it still fit. The hat was snug, but warm.

Being uncertain of the dress code for the evening, Todd called his mother. When she answered the phone, he asked, "Mom, what should I wear for Christmas singing with dogs?"

"Todd, slow down. I don't know what you mean."

Todd was accustomed to this complaint. He had been taught to break down his thoughts into multiple, more detailed sentences for those who didn't think the way he did. "I am going door-to-door singing with Laura and her parents tonight. We're going to sing Christmas songs."

"Todd, you can wear whatever you want when you go caroling. Just make sure you dress warmly."

Todd looked down at his worn jacket and work gloves. "I'm good."

He walked over and opened the door. "Mom, I'm letting Christmas out. He needs to stay with you tonight."

Mary Ann considered telling him to sing softly and

then reminded herself to just allow Todd to be Todd. "Have a really great time tonight. I love you." At the very last minute, she just couldn't control herself. "If you don't know the song real well, you should probably sing very softly."

"Thanks, Mom." Todd gathered up his coat and hurried out the door. The truck took a few minutes to warm up. When he was sure he had gas in the tank, his headlights were turned on, and no engine warning lights were flashing, he put the truck in gear and pulled out onto the highway, headed to town.

The drive was pleasant. Todd turned the radio on and listened to Christmas music. Just as Dolly Parton finished "Hard Candy Christmas," Todd pulled into the lot of the shelter. He ran inside, got Ranger and Mac, and returned to the truck with their ADOPT ME vests in hand.

When Todd arrived at Laura's house—the two canine sopranos in the cab with him—the small group of carolers was already gathered in the yard and warming up with "Oh, the weather outside is frightful, but the fire is so delightful. . . ."

Todd shook hands and exchanged introductions with the few relatives he did not already know, and then Laura's mother suggested the arrangement for the group. "Todd, you and the two dogs, in their wonderful vests, should stand at the front of the choir so that when our neighbors open their doors they'll be able to see Ranger and Mac and just want to keep them."

"Mom," Laura interjected, "it's not that easy."

Hearing no objection from Todd and ignoring Laura's plea to be more realistic about dog adoption, Mrs. Jordan gestured at Todd to go to the front of the group, and they headed down West Birch Street on a chilly December evening under a full moon.

Ginny and John Jordan, Laura's parents, sensed that Christmas caroling had become a bit dated, but every year it seemed like more and more people encouraged them to keep at it. As the holiday season neared, their friends and neighbors would approach them with the same message: "We don't have traditions anymore. I'm so glad your family does this."

John was skeptical. "They are just having so much fun laughing at us that they don't want us to stop."

Laura's mom asked the group, "Why don't we start with 'Silent Night, Holy Night'? That's an easy one." She looked at Todd. "Do you know that one?"

Todd had three versions of the song on his iPod playlist and knew it by heart. That was good; he would not have to sing softly because he knew the words. "I like that one. It's pretty good."

As they approached the first house, Ginny gave her instructions to Todd, "Just ring the doorbell, say 'Merry Christmas,' and then we start singing!"

So he would have at least one hand free, Ginny took the leash attached to the feisty little terrier, Ranger. Todd kept control of Mac's lead. Ranger was particularly pleased to be out on a stroll that night and was a tad unruly as he bounced about on the end of the leash.

They were standing near the steps of a yellow house with black shutters and a magnificent holly wreath hanging from the front door. Proudly perched on the three porch steps in ascending sizes were three Styrofoam snowmen outfitted with giant carrot noses and red button eyes. Juggling the leash and the song sheets in his left hand, Todd used his right hand to ring the doorbell. The carolers cleared their throats and waited for their cue.

From inside an elderly female voice that carried surprisingly well yelled from the kitchen, "Someone is at the door, Frank!"

"Well, answer it, Peggy!"

The carolers chuckled.

A woman in a blue robe peered out the door. She then yelled, "Come to the door, Frank! It's Ginny and John— Christmas caroling again."

"Do I have to?" the voice yelled back from the den, where the TV was blaring. "The Steelers are going for it on fourth and twelve. I can't miss this."

"Never mind!" she yelled back. The latch on the door slipped off and the door swung open. "Oh, what a treat! How nice to see you." She looked down. "Oh, my! And with dogs this time."

Todd shouted cheerfully, "Merry Christmas!"

The tenors opened with "Si-lent Night . . ."

The woman was taken with Ranger. She reached down and was greeted by the little terrier. "He's wonderful."

Ginny grabbed Peggy's arm affectionately and stopped singing long enough to try to close the sale. "He needs a home. Isn't he great?"

"Oh, but we already have a dog. Well, *I* do anyway—my sweet little girl. Still, Frank just loves terriers. He had one as a boy. I do wish he'd come to the door to see this fine fellow!"

Just then a little breeze blew the front door open all the way. Inside the house a small white teacup poodle, a tiny pink ribbon around her neck, got wind of the activity on *her* front porch. She stirred from her basket in the den, where she always seemed to be curled up sleeping if she wasn't yapping, and began her high-pitched barking as she charged from the den, down the hall, and through the open front door.

Ranger decided that he was fully up to the challenge and lunged at the dog. The pampered poodle turned tail and ran back inside. His valor challenged, Ranger gave chase, tugging his leash free from Ginny's hand.

Knowing a legitimate threat when she saw one, the poodle bolted down the hall, her toenails sounding like rapid gunfire on the polished wood floors. Ranger had the teacup poodle in his sights. Feeling the heat, the little white dog made a mad dash onto Frank's lap, from which vantage point she bared her gums and gave a menacing growl.

Frank yelled, "Peggy, there's a dog in the den!" He paused, noticing that his visitor was a terrier, and then turned up the volume to drown out the poodle's incessant yapping. *I bet* his *bark doesn't get old*, he thought.

Laura was giggling. Ginny was a bit worried that the little red-vested pooch was not behaving. Todd was not so bothered. He calmly observed, "Dogs do that." He handed Mac's leash to one of the other carolers, gave the "Sit" command, walked past the flustered Peggy into the hall, and called out, "Ranger, come!"

Wagging his tail, rather proud of his exploits, the little dog found Todd. Picking up the terrier's dangling leash, Todd led the dog out the front door, issuing another apology as he went. Ranger paused on the front steps.

By this time, the carolers had moved entirely off the porch and were huddled together chuckling on the sidewalk. Todd was not sure why they had not finished the song. Before he could make it down the steps to join them, Ranger lifted one leg. Now there was one yellow snowman and two white ones.

Peggy gave up. "Good night," she said to Ginny. "We'll see you next year."

Peggy shut the front door and watched the rest of the football game with her husband, cradling the shivering poodle in her lap. At halftime, Frank calmly observed, "That little terrier had spunk." He frowned at the poodle.

Todd pulled on the leash to encourage Ranger to move off the steps so he could get back to singing. Laura put her hand on her mother's shoulder to get her attention. "I don't think canine caroling is working out like we planned. I think it would be best if Todd takes the dogs back and you guys go ahead without us."

Ginny felt bad. "Are you sure?"

"Yes, Mom, I'm sure." She then turned to Todd. "Let's call it a night. Ranger is not a canine caroling kind of dog."

"Are you sure you don't want to try one more house with the dogs?" he asked.

From behind Todd everyone in the chorus gave a resounding "Yes!" Apparently, the idea of Ranger making another sneak attack on an unsuspecting neighbor was more than they could handle.

Laura knew that Todd would be slow to give up on any scheme that might help a dog find a home. "Not tonight, Todd. We tried. We still have a few weeks to find Ranger and Mac homes. We'll have to come up with another idea."

As the carolers approached the next house, Todd and Laura walked back to her home. They talked for a few minutes, and Laura let it be known that it had been a long day. "Will you call me tomorrow?"

Todd grinned. "It's a date." He got in his truck along with Mac and Ranger.

"Do you want me to help you take them back?" Laura asked.

"Thanks, but I can do it. Good night, Laura. Good night, Gracie."

Laura leaned in through the truck window and, without

a word, gave Todd a quick kiss on the cheek and turned away. Todd left the transmission in park until he was sure Laura and Gracie were safely inside.

He thought about Laura as he drove the half mile to the shelter and walked Mac and Ranger back to their pens. The cold air inside snapped him out of his reverie.

"Wow! It's cold in here." Todd walked over to the thermostat. "It's only forty degrees." Todd immediately called Hayley to let her know something was wrong with the heat.

Todd put Mac in his cage as he spoke to Hayley on his cell phone. "What should I do?"

Hayley checked her watch. At this late hour, it seemed unlikely that she would be able to find anyone to help her straighten out the furnace. Although it would be chilly for humans, the cold inside the shelter would not distress her furry guests. "They'll be fine for the night. We'll figure it out first thing tomorrow."

It was very quiet on the hospital wing of the Wellness Center, and pitch-black inside Hank Fisher's room except for the dim light coming through the crack under the door. It was slightly after midnight and he was not sure where he was or if he was even alone. Hank cleared his throat and said, "Is anyone here?"

No one answered. It had been a strange experience he

had awoken from. It must have been a dream. He was sitting at a T intersection in a blue-and-white GMC truck that he had not owned for twenty years. Summer was in full flower, exploding in grainy Technicolor. The corn was tall but still a tender green. The truck engine was idling. He felt lost; he did not know if he should turn west or east.

A white dog appeared from behind a tree located along the edge of an adjacent cornfield. The dog walked slowly to the west, stopped, looked back to Hank, and trotted down the road. Hank put his turn signal on, turned right, and followed the dog west down the gravel road. They moved slowly for half a mile at a relaxed pace. There were occasional farmhouses along the road. Following a curve in the road, Hank passed through a stand of timber. At the bottom of a hill he crossed over an old wooden bridge that rattled gently under the weight of his truck. The road ended and the dog disappeared back into the woods.

Hank pulled the covers around him and fell back asleep, hoping to travel again in the comfort of the same dream. He wanted to get back to the dog, to see where he was leading him.

Later, but still in the early morning hours, the outside temperature dipped into the lower teens. The wind swung to the north. The temperature inside the shelter fell below thirty-two. The animals weren't bothered. It was pleasant enough for them. The water in the pipes that ran throughout the shelter slowly grew ice-cold. Around 3:15 that morning the first pipe burst. A cascading spray of water shot across the shelter. By dawn three more pipes had burst, and even more water began rushing through the shelter. As the water accumulated, the guests became unhappy with their accommodations.

CHAPTER 15

HAYLEY ARRIVED at the shelter a little after 7:30 that morning. Given the way things had been going over the last few weeks, it seemed fitting that part of the ceiling had collapsed in her office, water was streaming across the floors, and ice was accumulating on the walls and floor. *What else? Why me?* These questions played in her head like a catchy jingle for some product she definitely didn't need. Trying to keep her shoes dry, she gingerly crossed over the rivulets of water that ran down the aisles between the cages in the shelter. Her office area was inaccessible, her desk buried beneath an eight-foot segment of water-soaked Sheetrock. She made her way to the utility closet, immediately turned the water supply valve off, and called the city manager.

By 8:15 Hayley had Mayor McDaniel, the city manager, the gas company representative, and the furnace man at the shelter piecing together what had happened. Their coats were tightly wrapped around them. No one wanted to take responsibility for the colossal mess, but in fact it wasn't anyone's fault. It turned out that the gas had not been shut off; the ancient furnace had simply given out.

Hayley shook her head and said, "It doesn't matter what happened. We just have to get it repaired and get this mess cleaned up."

"Give us a minute, Hayley," Mayor McDaniel said.

The mayor, city manager, and gas rep spoke to the furnace man about their options. The four of them wandered about the shelter inspecting the mess. Shaking their heads despondently, they returned to Hayley and tried to calmly tell her what they hoped she could figure out on her own. The city manager took the lead.

"There is no way we're going to get this mess cleaned up without spending a lot of money. The city doesn't have tens of thousands of dollars to repair an old furnace and clean up a building that is about to be demolished. I'm sorry, Hayley, but this shelter is done with, as far as we're concerned. You need to find a different place for the dogs you have left or call Doc Pelot and just put them down. Those are the only options we see."

The mayor knew this was tough medicine for Hayley to swallow. "If you have some better idea, we'll consider it. Otherwise, what else can we do?"

Hayley's face was flushed. With a scowl, she asked the mayor, "How about we put them in your garage?"

Mayor Annie McDaniel understood Hayley's bitterness and tried not to respond in kind. It would do no good to tell Hayley that she was two months late on her mortgage, that she was doing everything in her power to solve the city's financial problems, and that she cared as much about these animals as the next person.

"Hayley, we're on the same team, you and me, so please don't be mad. This stinks, but it's not as if the city broke the furnace or told the county to sell the shelter grounds and building right out from underneath us. We're struggling through this, but it's just the crisis of the day for me. You're the shelter manager, so I need you to find a solution."

Hayley glared at her. "Like what?"

"How about one of those other shelters that you were trying to put on standby—the ones in Kansas City? Maybe they can take these last few stragglers?"

About that time Todd and Christmas walked through the front door. Todd's face was wrinkled with worry. "Was it an ice tornado?"

"It wasn't a tornado, but it sure looks like it." Hayley was happy to see Todd and his dog. "The furnace broke and the pipes froze and burst. That's what caused the mess."

"Should I start cleaning up?" Todd asked his boss.

Hayley walked over to Todd and, more for her own benefit than his, gave him a hug. She took a step back, but continued to clutch his shoulders with her hands. "Todd, we can't operate out of the shelter anymore. We have no water or heat. This mess would take days, if not weeks, to clean up. The city has no money to fix this. We can't let the public come in here to see our dogs in these conditions. We're going to have to shut down a little earlier than planned. We have no other choice. I'm sorry."

In the kennel area, twelve cold and wet abandoned dogs were shivering. The last two cats were still with the merchants on Main Street who had adopted them for the holidays. *It was just as well; they would have hated being wet,* Hayley thought.

She knew that Todd had been training and caring for the dogs, diligently trying so hard to place each dog in a loving home. The animals deserved no less.

Todd asked the logical question: "If they don't live here, then where do we put them all? Ranger, Gertie, Past Due, Mac, Bird Dog, Tommy Lee, Willy, and the other ones— where will they live?"

Hayley's voice cracked as she asked, "Todd, do you remember our Plan B? That's what we have to do."

"The other shelters?"

"Yes. That's what we'll have to do."

"I don't like Plan B. You know I don't like how other shelters operate, and neither do you. They don't treat the animals like we do. . . ." He grew silent, clearly thinking about the possibility that the dogs might be put down at shelters that didn't embrace a no-kill policy.

Hayley wanted so badly to set an example of strength, but this was too much. She couldn't bury her hurt and frustration as she tried again to explain. "Todd, they can't stay here. Look at them. They're miserable. We can't care for them here—not anymore. In another shelter, one that is open to the public, someone might adopt them. We just can't keep them. Not here."

"I trained Ranger and Bird Dog and all the rest of them. They're good animals. I can find them homes. I can do it," he insisted.

Hayley had no idea what more she could say. Todd seemed incapable of facing reality—and no doubt he didn't want to. She turned away and suppressed a scream. Todd's idealism was a double-edged sword. He could lift everyone's spirits so high with his optimism, but in situations like this, when he refused to accept the truth, he could drive his friends and family to distraction.

Annie McDaniel felt like sinking into one of the half-frozen puddles of water that had accumulated on the concrete floor. "Todd?" she asked gently, "what do you think we should do?"

The mayor was soliciting ideas for a long-term solution, but Todd could not get past the more immediate crisis. He looked around at the shelter. "First, we have to get them into dry cages." Todd turned, walked a few steps, opened the supply closet door, and found a stack of towels. "Let's dry them off."

After the dogs were dried and consolidated, Todd walked them back to the three dry cages. Scooping what dry dog chow she could find into feeding bowls, Hayley made sure everyone was fed. It seemed to her that Todd was stunned. She stepped aside and quietly called George on the phone. She told the elder McCray what had happened and the plan to move the animals to another shelter. "Todd seems to be having a hard time accepting that the shelter has been destroyed," she said. "Staying here is not an option."

George was not surprised. "I'll be there in fifteen minutes." He called Mary Ann and, after bringing her up to date on the shelter mess, he asked her if she could leave school for an hour and join him at the shelter so they could speak to Todd together.

It was the last school day before the winter break and not much was happening. She said, "See you there," and hung up the phone.

"You old buzzard," Doc Pelot called out from the doorway of Hank's hospital room, "can I come in?"

"Do I have a choice?"

"Nope."

"Then get it over with."

Doc Pelot approached Hank's bedside leaning on his walnut cane. He moved closer to Hank and spoke to him in a more serious tone. "The nurse just told me you are doing much better today. How are you feeling?"

"I'd like to get out of this bed and move around. Maybe in a few days. We'll see."

"Can you walk?"

"Doctor Wilson said I can give it a try this afternoon if I'm still feeling better."

Doc Pelot was so pleased. "Hank, old friend, we were beginning to question whether you would ever return to the land of the living. If you were that tired of playing gin rummy with me, you could have just said so."

"I do get tired of losing to you." The grin left Hank's face and he continued, "It has been a strange few days. When I woke, I felt lost."

"I'm glad you found your way back, Hank." Doc Pelot put his hand out and rested it on Hank's arm. "You may have picked a good time to check out. While you were sleeping, things have been a little crazy around here."

"My cows?" Hank asked.

"No, your cows are fine. George has been taking good care of them. No, this is something else. The pipes froze at the shelter last night. The mayor and the city manager are over there now. I just left. It's a mess. They can't wait until the first of the year to close the shelter. It has to close now. We're going to have to step up and figure something out."

Hank looked at his friend and felt surprised, first, and aggravated, second. He allowed himself to sink further down in the bed. "It sounds like that twenty grand I gave them a few years back to fix up the building was money down the drain. That makes it harder for me to dig in and help again. I tell you, Doc, every time I get sick, this town falls apart."

"So quit getting sick."

"Fair enough. I'll do what I can. What are we going to do without a shelter?"

Doc Pelot slowly lowered himself into one of the guest chairs. "You and I are too old to be running a shelter, Hank. It's time for the next generation in this community to step up. Otherwise, it's going to be like the bad old days around here again."

Hank and Doc Pelot were old enough to remember how unwanted domestic animals had lived before the county shelter was opened, and it was not a time they cared to relive. Abandoned dogs, often traveling in dangerous packs, wandered around starving, rummaging through trash and eating whatever they could find. Desperately hungry, they often got into the feed meant for farm animals or went after the animals themselves, killing chickens, pestering livestock, and more times than not ending up on the receiving end of some farmer's or rancher's bullet. Without the free spaying and neutering the shelter offered, cats turned feral, causing problems as they reproduced unchecked and their numbers swelled.

Neglected animals spread illnesses, and, just as bad, the poor creatures became sick themselves; or, left to make their own way with little chance of survival, they suffered debilitating injuries. Neglected when they most needed human help, they suffered unnecessarily.

It was sad, but before their community had a shelter, that was the way it had been. For these two animal lovers, it looked as if the clock might be turned back and once again any unwanted pets would suffer a sorry fate.

Hank shook his head. "I don't want those old days. What are we going to do?"

"We need to talk about it," the vet answered.

"Start talking then."

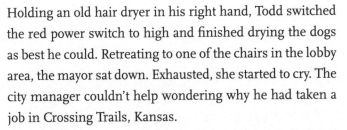

Holding an old hair dryer in his right hand, Todd switched the red power switch to high and finished drying the dogs as best he could. Retreating to one of the chairs in the lobby area, the mayor sat down. Exhausted, she started to cry. The city manager couldn't help wondering why he had taken a job in Crossing Trails, Kansas.

George pulled out of the driveway and headed toward Crossing Trails, traveling as fast as he reasonably could. By the time he and Mary Ann arrived at the shelter, the city manager and the mayor had left. George tapped on Mary Ann's car window.

She opened the car door and got out. "Let's get this over with."

There was a glaze of ice on the front door of the shelter. After timidly pushing it open, Mary Ann looked about, shocked. "All this damage from frozen pipes?"

George had seen it happen before and knew what a mess burst pipes could make. He stepped around piles of fallen debris and called out, "Todd?" Hearing no answer, he and Mary Ann negotiated their way back to the kennel area, where they found Hayley trying to set up the propane space heaters that the mayor's husband had dropped by on his way to work.

When she saw George, she yelled out, "Be careful, the wet floor is slippery!"

George moved cautiously forward with Mary Ann holding his arm. Concerned for his son, George asked, "Where's Todd?"

"He's outside in the exercise area with Ranger and Christmas. He'll be back in a few minutes. Mr. and Mrs. McCray, you're going to have to help me with him."

"How?" Mary Ann asked.

"We're out of options. You need to help Todd understand that the shelter is closed. *Now.* We will have to transport the last twelve dogs to other shelters. I've called around, and we can make it happen today. Todd had it in his head that he could find adoptive families for all of them. We got close, but it's too late. He knows these other shelters aren't like ours. I think he's going to have a hard time with this."

"We'll do what we can," Mary Ann said, tightening her grip on George's arm for support.

At that moment, Todd walked through the side door with Ranger and Christmas, both dogs oblivious to the disaster around them and simply excited to be with Todd on a brief outdoor romp.

George looked at Todd, who was smiling and calm despite the circumstances. On so many days, like this one, he wondered if the world fully appreciated his son. His shelter universe was literally collapsing around him. Still, he just kept doing what had to be done. Todd sank to his knees so both dogs could nestle their noses under his chin and deliver their affectionate message of gratitude for his care.

Suddenly he stood up. "Watch this!" He moved his flat hand horizontally across his chest. Suddenly, he dropped it vertically to complete an L-shaped gesture. "Sit."

Like synchronized swimmers, both dogs sat. "Good job." Todd reached into his pocket and gave both Ranger and Christmas a training treat.

George knew that the world wouldn't care much if a dozen dogs in a small town in Kansas made it or not, but their fate would make a world of difference to his son. If Todd was a gift to the world, then from time to time the world could darn well make a gift back to Todd. George saw that he had something to give. He could give a gift that really mattered. George bent down and had an imaginary conversation with Christmas. With the discussion completed, he looked first at Mary Ann and then at Todd.

"You would never believe what this dog of ours just told me," he said with great seriousness.

Todd smiled. It was not the first time George had played this game with him. On many occasions Christmas had "told" Todd he needed to clean his room or do some other chore he'd been neglecting.

"What did he say this time, Dad?" Todd asked, playing along.

George crouched down again, pretending to receive a canine communiqué. "What's that, boy? Okay, I'll tell them. This old dog says that your shelter friends need a home for Christmas."

"They can't stay here, Dad. It's too big a mess." Todd made a sweeping gesture indicating the havoc of their surroundings.

George put his hand under the black Lab's jaw and tilted his head up so that he could see into the dog's green eyes. "Christmas knows that, so he says your dogs should stay with us—in the barn—until you can find homes for them. This dog of ours is pretty smart, don't you think?"

Todd bent down and whispered loudly to Ranger. "What? Say it again." Todd stood up and delivered his own dog message. "Ranger thinks you and Christmas are smart. We better get started moving them."

Hayley smiled for the first time all morning. Mary Ann nodded in agreement.

George discussed with Hayley and Todd what needed to be done. It seemed to Mary Ann like a tremendous amount of work, but she went along with the plan. They would have to disassemble and reassemble at least a dozen cages, move food and supplies, and provide care for a dozen animals until a permanent solution could be found.

Mary Ann returned to school while George and Todd drove back to the McCray farm for tools and supplies. Needing something with ample space to haul cages, dogs, and supplies, George hitched his truck to his four-horse trailer.

Mary Ann headed straight to the principal's office and thanked Principal Wallace for covering her eleventh-grade debate class.

"No problem. Reminded me why I don't teach anymore!" the principal remarked.

When he asked about the outcome of her emergency mission, Mary Ann gave him a rundown.

He moved to the edge of his chair. "Sounds to me like the shelter could use some help today."

"George has no idea what he has gotten himself into," Mary Ann said. "We'll do the best we can."

"I've got an idea. Follow me." Principal Wallace went to the front reception desk and elbowed his way past a covey of students providing various excuses for being late or leaving early. He picked up the microphone for the PA system and pressed a button. The halls and classroom were suddenly interrupted by a little horn-like sound, the harbinger of an announcement from the front office.

"This is Principal Wallace. Sorry to interrupt your studies, but I have an important announcement." Stan Wallace was pretty sure that what he was about to do violated multiple school board and state policies. He also figured that everyone should and would look the other way this time. He'd been at that town meeting, and if this wasn't an opportunity for folks to pull together—and a chance for the younger citizens in town to get involved—then what was? If anyone complained, he'd give them an earful about teachable moments.

"Pipes burst and created a mess out at our animal shelter. I need five volunteers to help move some animals and set up a temporary shelter out at Mrs. McCray's farm. This will count as an excused absence. If you're caught up with your work and if you're interested in helping, please come to my office."

Within minutes there was a steady stream of students rushing to the front office. He chose the five he had the most confidence in, collected them in his office, and gave them instructions.

"You have to contact your parents first. You can't leave until they call the office and give their permission. Once Mrs. Randolph tells me you've been cleared, then you can go home and change into work clothes. Also if you can borrow a few hand tools from your parents that would be nice. My guess is hammers and crowbars would be best for taking apart cages and putting them back together again. Try to be over at the shelter in half an hour."

Back at the shelter George suggested that they disassemble and move sixteen pens, even though they were down to only twelve dogs—just in case someone showed up with another stray or two. Within a few hours, after multiple trips back and forth, sixteen pens had been taken apart and put back together in the McCrays' barn using lumber and materials that were recycled from the shelter. All of the food and supplies had been moved into the old milking pens. Straw lined the cages, and the barn's old furnace was at least taking an edge off the cold air.

By early evening all of the dogs seemed comfortably situated. Three of the dogs had a very short stay in their newly assigned cages. In fact, they had already moved on to new homes. Each one had been looked over one last time by a Crossing Trails High volunteer, a decision was made, paperwork was quickly completed, and a car door was shut. In the dim light of the setting sun, each of the students set off with their new pet in the backseat of an old car.

An hour earlier, after a hard afternoon of work, each of the three students had called home to their parents to make their pleas. "Mom, I've got to bring this dog home!" There was surprisingly little objection. Given the shelter's plight and the enthusiasm in their child's voice, it was hard to say no.

Todd's cell phone had been busily ringing all day.

Frustrated by the interruptions, he turned off the ringer. It was dinnertime before he remembered to turn it back on. He had three messages from Laura. She was worried about him and wanted him to call her right away. Hayley wanted to talk to him about dividing up the work at their new emergency location, and Ed Lee wanted to know if Todd would like to become an employee of Paradise Valley Farms. His message was very kind: "Todd, the other two people that interviewed did not measure up to you. I think you could really add to our operations. You can start after Christmas or the first of the year, whichever you prefer. Call me back in the next week and let me know if you want the job." Ed Lee seemed anxious to fill the position.

Todd got out of his voice mail and joined his father, who was relaxing against the swinging door to a horse stall, staring out over the temporary shelter and trying to decide if this was the single craziest thing he had ever done in his life. While he was sure there were probably less prudent things he had done, none came to mind.

"Dad?"

"Yes, Todd."

"Looks like we both have new jobs."

George was getting ready to launch into a speech about this being Todd's responsibility. He was providing the space, nothing more, but there was something about the little smile on Todd's face that caused him to pause and ask, "What do you mean?"

"You're the new assistant shelter manager, and they offered me a spot at the dairy."

George shook his son's hand and then pulled him into an embrace. "Congratulations, son, I'm very proud of you. They're lucky to have you."

While Todd and George put away tools and did a final inspection of the temporary shelter, Mary Ann pulled together a quick dinner and called them into the house to join her. Todd was so tired he could hardly hold his head up as he ate. His explanation about the dairy job was very brief, and although Mary Ann tried to get more details, he was clearly too exhausted for conversation. After quietly demolishing an oversized bowl of chocolate ice cream, he left for Thorne's cabin.

George moved to the living room, and Mary Ann removed a tablecloth and dishes from the hutch in the dining room and began preparing the table for their weekend holiday party. As there was only a half wall separating the dining room space from the living room space, they talked freely back and forth.

"Don't you think Todd seems sort of close-mouthed about the dairy? He didn't seem to want to talk about it, though I know he was tired. Do you think he's nervous?" she asked while rolling red and green cloth napkins and slipping them inside small pinecone napkin holders.

"It's got to be a little scary for him. He didn't say much

to me, either. Just that he got hired. His mind is probably still on the shelter. Today was a tough one."

"Do you think the dairy will work out for him?"

"Sure it will, but I was thinking that in some ways working there will be Todd's first real job."

"The shelter was a real job. What do you mean?" Mary Ann asked.

"At the dairy he's going to be asked to do things that are hard and that don't come easily to him, not like at the shelter."

"I'm not sure I follow." She hesitated, uncomfortable with what George was saying. "What kind of things?"

"Don't you have to do things at the school—maybe it's a particularly unpleasant parent-teacher conference—that you would just as soon pass on?"

"I guess, but I enjoy ninety-nine percent of being a teacher, and it gives me very little comfort to think he is going to have to do things he doesn't enjoy or that are 'unpleasant.' I'm not sure why you see such tasks as some wonderful growth experience for him."

George knew this talk was headed in a direction he did not want to go. "That's not what I said. My point is that Todd is entitled to feel a little nervous and to hesitate; this is going to be a brand-new world for him."

George knew that Mary Ann was concerned, maybe even a little upset, and that was why she was being testy. "He'll be fine." George glanced over the top of his newspaper and waited for her to respond.

She asked, "Fine?" With a hard edge on the *n*.

Trying to imitate the emphasis, George said, "Yes, he'll be fi*ne*. How about you, Mary Ann. Will you be fi*ne*?"

She looked up from her work. "I'm feeling a little shell-shocked, to be honest."

George set the paper down. "There's a lot going on. Todd's new job, the shelter, the holidays are almost here—it's a lot on him. Why don't you take a break? Come over here and sit down with me."

Mary Ann did not argue. Instead, she settled in beside him on the living room couch. Trying to reassure her, George remarked, "I hope the dairy will work out for Todd, we'll find homes for this last bunch of stragglers, and things will get back to normal with the New Year."

"Agreed, but now that he has the dairy position, maybe he'll want to move to Crossing Trails?"

He looked over his glasses and said to his wife, *"Could be."*

The two words, however, communicated much more. They were spoken with a certain patience, love, and resignation that seemed to go to the core of what Mary Ann had been struggling with the last few weeks. "Could be" was George's gentle way of reminding Mary Ann that Todd had his own future. He was growing up. They needed to let go.

"So that's it. 'Could be' is all you have to say." She had to laugh. She knew her husband was trying his hardest to help her work through all of it, and she wanted him to know that at the end of the day, she agreed. They would all get through it. She also suspected that behind all of George's patient letting-go dialogue was a great big heaping dose of denial. If Todd moved to Crossing Trails, he would be just as worried as she would be.

Mary Ann pulled the glasses off George's face and kissed him gently on the nose. Nestling her chin under his ear, she whispered, "The perfect way for me to stop fussing over Todd would be for me to spend a lot more time fussing over you. Would you mind?"

George immediately stood up and gave a long yawn. "I think it's time for bed. Todd will be just *fine*."

At the bottom of McCray's Hill, in Thorne's cabin, Todd sat at the kitchen table and read his e-mails. There was one from Julie at the Heartland School for Dogs. He read it twice to make sure he understood. He tried Laura again. The line had been busy the last two times he had tried to call. This time he got through.

"Where have you been?" Laura asked.

"I've been very busy. A lot happened today—there's so much to tell you, Laura."

Todd told her about the broken pipes, the shelter's emergency closing, and how convenient it was having all of the dogs in his own barnyard.

She listened with great interest, but all the while she

was hesitant to ask him a question, out of fear that the answer would not be good, but finally she could not resist. "Did you hear from the dairy?"

"Yes, they offered me the job. They must have liked me. I'm good with cows." He paused and then added, "I'd rather work with dogs. You can't train cows. I don't know if I want to take it."

"I was just thinking, maybe you should not rush into it. Who knows if something else might come up for you? Why don't you take a week or so to think about it?"

"That's what I'm going to talk to you about."

"Now?"

"Yes, I sent an e-mail to Julie Bradshaw at Heartland, the dog-training place. She wrote me back." Todd moved over to the computer. "I think I better read it to you. Here goes:"

> Todd,
> Thanks so much for writing. I'm glad you enjoyed the training video. I'm really bummed about your shelter closing, but I might have good news for you. We have an opening here at Heartland for an assistant service-dog trainer! It's a three-year program, and we train the employee; after you complete the program, you'll be considered a professional service-dog trainer. We've interviewed several people already

and need to make a decision soon. Personally,
I think you'd be a good fit for it, but of course
you'd have to interview like everyone else.
Would you be interested in driving up here so
we can talk about it? If so, call me right away so
I can set up an interview with our director.

    Julie Bradshaw
    Director of Canine Development

    Todd waited for Laura to say something. When she didn't, he wondered if he had lost his cell phone connection—a frequent occurrence in rural Cherokee County. "Laura, are you still there?" he asked.

    Laura felt like she was leaning over the edge of a cliff. She gripped the bedspread in her right hand and pulled Gracie closer to her. She felt so many things at once: proud, afraid, hurt, worried, and joyful. She had no idea what to say. All the emotions were swirling around, and it would take days for her and Todd to sort them out. Right now, the confusion just produced tears. She pushed them back. "I'm here, Todd. I'm here."

CHAPTER 16

THE FIRST sip of his morning coffee always tasted the best. George folded the paper and left it on the kitchen table for Mary Ann and quickly finished the rest of the cup. The back porch light barely pierced the fog that hugged the snow-crusted ground.

Christmas had begun renegotiating his custody arrangement between George and Todd. Now that he was not going into work with Todd every day at the shelter, he was spending a lot of his time with George and Mary Ann. George opened the door and let him back in after the Lab's morning constitutional. There was a howling north wind, and Christmas scooted back inside and regained his favorite spot by the fire. George rinsed his cereal bowl, put it in the dishwasher, and walked into the mudroom to put on his coat, gloves, and boots.

As part of his morning routine, George tore the page

off the calendar—Friday, December 20th—and put it in the trash can. Another year was approaching its final lap. It seemed like it had been only a few weeks ago that he had hung this year's calendar and pulled off January 1. George opened the back door and started digging in his pockets for truck keys, walking through the cold, damp air. He drove through the winter morning darkness to Hank's farm and did the milking. When he finished that he returned home, checked on the mostly sleeping shelter dogs, and did his own chores. Todd joined him for an hour to help and then hurried off on some important but undefined errand.

With his work complete, George sat down for a mid-morning cup of coffee with Mary Ann. It was just two days before the annual McCray holiday party, so she was too busy to linger. She was rinsing her cup and putting it away when the phone rang. It was Louisa Sailor.

"Just wanted you to know how excited we are about coming to your party Sunday evening," Mary Ann's friend said.

"Well, Louisa, George and I are glad you and Rick can make it."

There was a pause, and it was obvious to Mary Ann that something else was on her friend's mind. She tried to speed the conversation to its conclusion. "I guess we'll see you Sunday?"

"Just one more thing. And, Mary Ann, I just thought you should know this, and I hope you don't think I'm being a gossip. . . ."

Knowing Louisa to be just that, Mary Ann prodded her. "Go ahead, Louisa, what is it?"

"Well, your son, Todd, just left the bank. We were both the first ones in this morning." The woman paused to make sure that her startling revelation had time to fully register. "So I just happened to be behind him waiting for a teller and, again, I know it's none of my business. But, Mary Ann, I think you'll be quite surprised to learn that Todd closed his savings account and they gave him thirty-two hundred and twenty-four dollars and sixteen cents in cash. He left with all that money in his pocket. Walked right out of the bank like it was a perfectly normal thing to do! Now, I just thought to myself, what does Todd McCray need with that much money? Mother to mother, I thought you should know."

Mary Ann sighed. "Louisa, thanks for calling. I will check into it." She hung up and tried to avoid speculating on why her son needed that much money. She tried to tell herself, for the third time that day, to stop worrying about Todd. George was right. He was fine.

She sat back down with her husband and tried to make light of the call from her nosy friend. "That was Louisa Sailor, who saw your son at the bank this morning. She thinks that Todd is running away and joining the French Foreign Legion."

Mary Ann told him the entire story. The telling only made it worse. Eventually she gave up the pretext of not worrying. "I'm concerned. What's this about?"

George offered what comfort he could. "Todd is pretty careful with his money."

"Still, why that much and what for?"

"I honestly don't know."

She abruptly stood up from the table and began to pace about the kitchen. "I'm sorry but I can't just sit around and not worry about this," she said, with increasing anxiety in her voice. "Maybe you can, but I'm not that good. We're going to have to get to the bottom of it."

"He's over twenty-one and it's his money. It's Christmastime. . . ." George caught himself in the middle of the thought. The pieces started to come together. Todd had been asking him about the nature of good gift giving. He had been expressing his love for Laura. *No,* he told himself. *Surely not.* He wasn't ready for another daughter-in-law, and Todd was not ready for a wife. While he wondered about the withdrawal of the money, George decided not to voice any wild theories. "I'll check into it," he told Mary Ann.

He picked up the phone and dialed Todd's number. Todd answered on the second ring and seemed preoccupied. "What's up?" Todd asked.

"Nothing much. Say, Todd, I was wondering—how is your money situation? Are you a little worried about not having a job? You've got lots in savings, right?"

"Don't worry, Dad. I've got plenty of money. Also, Laura and I will be gone all day tomorrow, back late. We've got something special planned. Got to go!"

Todd's secretive behavior only added to his parents'

worries. It also didn't help that Todd had been spending an extraordinary amount of time on the phone with Laura over the last two weeks.

On the following Saturday morning, Mary Ann rose earlier than normal. George had left over an hour earlier for Hank's farm to do the early-morning milking. The Christmas party was the next day, and while she still had a few things left to do, her worries were centered on Todd and his sudden need for cash.

Mary Ann walked over to the window. The sun was up far enough in the morning sky for her to see Todd's truck still parked in his driveway. When she had gone to bed the night before, just after eleven, Laura's car had still been parked in the cabin's gravel driveway. She knew Laura's parents would not be happy about her driving home that late at night. Neither was she.

She sat down in her chair, drank her coffee, and thought about her son. When George got back, she let loose. "I just can't stand it another minute."

"What's wrong?"

"You have to go down there and see what's going on with Todd."

"What do you mean?"

"George! Demand an explanation. You let him off too easy."

There was no use arguing. "I'll be back in a few minutes," George said.

When he arrived at Thorne's cabin, George opened the

door and called out for Todd, but there was no answer. It was only 7:15, but Todd was a very early riser, and George expected him to be awake. George called out again. "Todd, are you up?"

When his son emerged from his bedroom, George was stunned. "What happened to Todd McCray? There's some handsome guy standing in his cabin wearing a suit!"

"Dad," Todd moaned. "It's me. Todd McCray."

George whistled. "Wow, that outfit must have set you back a few dollars."

"It did. Do you like it?"

Todd turned around. His tie was knotted like a lead line on a spring heifer and hung clumsily from his neck.

"I love the suit," George said. "The tie is perfect, but I can help you tie a smaller knot. I'm not sure about the socks and shoes."

Todd looked down at his white socks and red Converse tennis shoes. "That's what I wanted to ask you about. I bought new ones." He motioned over to the box on the sofa. "But I kind of like these better. What do you think?"

"Why don't you try the new ones on for me? They'll look better with those black socks." George pointed to the pair of dark socks resting by the shoes.

Todd put them on, stood up, and said, "They still feel funny."

"They always do at first. You're just not used to the hard soles."

"So do you think I should wear them?"

"You bought them for a reason. Right?" George was itching to find out what that reason was—and why Todd had closed his savings account and where he was going that morning. But he also far preferred that Todd tell him in his own way and in his own good time. *Patience*, he thought to himself, thankful that he'd been the one to come upon this scene and not Mary Ann.

Todd held his right leg up, so he could give his shoes a closer inspection. "I guess they fit." He then took off the necktie and handed it to George. "I didn't know how to tie it."

George motioned his son over to the mirror that hung beside the picture he had recently hung nearby, the one of Grandpa Bo carrying George on his shoulders. He stepped behind Todd, tied the knot for his son, and slipped the tie snuggly against his collar. "What do you think?" George asked.

"I look pretty handsome."

"Any particular reason you want to look so handsome?" he pressed, ever so gently.

"Laura and I have a special day planned today."

"I see," George said casually, straightening the shirt's collar.

Once again, George was glad he was the one here, and not Mary Ann. He didn't want to speculate on how she'd react to *Laura and I have a special day planned.*

It was obvious to George that Todd was still avoiding coming right out and saying what he was doing. George wanted to respect Todd's privacy and to follow his own advice about not meddling in Todd's life. Still, he hoped Todd was not doing something he would later regret. George was trying hard to balance that uneasiness with his desire to let Todd make his own choices.

"If you need a hand, you know where to find me." George looked down at the pile of Todd's old discarded clothing on the floor, punctuated by his red Converse tennis shoes. "We'll see you tomorrow at the open house?"

"I'll be there. I've called Hayley. She's coming out later this morning to feed, water, and exercise the dogs, but I'll be back later today, except it might be a little late."

"Sounds good, Todd. You're okay, right?"

"Sure."

"Nothing you want to tell me?"

Todd was nonchalant. "Dad, don't worry. I'm good."

Todd felt awkward driving in the suit. Once in Crossing Trails, he went straight to Laura's house and parked his truck. They decided it was safer and more comfortable to drive her car. Julie had suggested that bringing Gracie would showcase Todd's skills far better than any résumé. "Gracie is a walking, breathing demonstration of your skill and accomplishments," Julie had said. "You should bring her. If she doesn't mind the drive, we'd love to meet your Laura, too."

It was close to a three-hour drive to Washington, Kansas—a town in so many ways just like Crossing Trails, and the home of the Heartland School for Dogs. They were on the road by eight. Todd used the GPS app on his cell phone to retrieve a map and exact directions. The trip took him and Laura north past Manhattan, Kansas, and through the beautiful flint hills that rose from the prairie like gentle sphinxes.

Julie and her boss, Lyle Hanks, would meet them for a tour and then they would go to lunch together and talk some more about the school.

❄

George was doing his best to calm Mary Ann down, but it was not going well.

"So all you know is he bought a suit and they're going to spend the day together. George, something is up. Todd took all his money out of the bank. Do you think they're going to do something crazy like elope and move to France?"

"That idea did occur to me. Not a bad plan." He took his wife's hands in his own. "Would you like to elope with me and move to France? I make a mean grilled *fromage*."

She thrust his hands aside. "George, this is no time to joke."

"You're worrying too much. It's Christmastime. Todd was asking me about gift-giving. Maybe they're driving to Kansas City and he's treating her to a nice day on the town."

Worry returned to her face. "A three-thousand-dollar nice day on the town, dressed in a suit? How do you spend that much money in Kansas City?"

"Mary Ann, he is a twenty-four-year-old man entitled to do what he wants with his own money. We're going to have to trust him. We'll know soon enough."

Todd had never been to Disneyland. The Heartland School for Dogs was the next best thing. He more floated than walked through Heartland's facilities with a strong sense of having arrived at some crucial place on his life path. The buildings and kennels were spotlessly clean. Hayley would have approved.

On a good day at the shelter, Todd might have an hour or two to really work on training dogs. Most of his time was spent caring for and feeding the animals. Here the priorities were different. The dogs at Heartland were not waiting in pens hoping to find a place to call home—a place where they could belong and be accepted. Dogs were the kings at the Heartland School. Because they had a purpose and a calling, they enthusiastically embraced each day of their lives.

Julie couldn't resist pulling one of her favorite goldens out of the kennel. As she briefly worked Lily, any observer would be able to see that a sense of purpose emanated from the very core of her canine soul; the retriever was focused and happy to do her job. Like the dog he was watching, Todd was nearly overwhelmed with joy. He felt more at home than when he was at home. He just kept saying, "Wow!" Laura could feel his excitement and reached out to squeeze his hand.

After the tour Julie asked Todd to show Lyle some of the things that he had taught Gracie. They went into a huge training room that was filled with props—wheelchairs, mannequins, pull toys, and boxes of objects to be identified and retrieved. Todd shot for the moon. He recognized the room from the training video. He looked around until he found what he was searching for. He took the lead from Laura and walked Gracie out into the center of the room. He faced west, said her name softly to get her attention, and gave the first of many commands.

"Refrigerator!"

Gracie sprang into action. For the next ten minutes, she executed command after command. She was flawless.

And so was Todd.

After Todd completed his demonstration with Gracie, Lyle ushered him into his office, where he conducted the formal interview for the next hour. Julie knew enough to make her decision, so she spent the time with Laura talking about Laura's work with Gracie in the Wellness Center.

When he was finished, Lyle ordered in lunch—sub sandwiches magically delivered from right across the street—and they all ate together in the facility's dining space, which was located in one corner of the large training room.

Lyle eased into what amounted to his only remaining concern. "Todd, to become certified as a service-dog trainer takes most of our new employees three years. It's like a college degree. Except with us, you do the work and don't read about how to do it. You're way ahead of where we expect most new hires to be, so it might not take that long for you. Still, it's a big commitment."

Todd was comfortable enough to be honest. "I learn better doing and not reading."

Lyle put it out there: "Is this something you want? Are you willing to make a three-year commitment?"

"Yes, sir, it's something I want. More than anything."

Lyle glanced at Julie, who nodded. "In that case, Todd, let us talk and we'll try to get right back to you."

CHAPTER 17

TODD DROPPED his keys on his kitchen table and checked his cell phone for messages. There were several—all from the same person. He hurriedly dialed the number.

"Hi, Mom—got your messages."

"I've been calling you all day."

"Sorry, I muted the ringer and forgot to turn it back on." Todd felt a little guilty after hearing her worried tone on his voice mail.

"So are you home now?" Mary Ann asked.

"Yes. Do you want me to come to the back door and wave at you?" He wasn't sure what he'd say if she asked him where he'd been all day, so he was relieved when she didn't ask.

"No, I just wanted to make sure you were okay." She was dying to know where he'd disappeared to, but she was trying very hard to follow George's suggestion and leave

Todd alone. "I'm glad you're home. I need to finish getting ready for the party."

"I'll come up to the house in a few minutes to help out."

He's safe, that's all that matters, and that's all I need to know for now, Mary Ann told herself as she hung up. She willed herself to relax and finish her last-minute party preparations. It was just after six on Sunday when the first cars started to arrive.

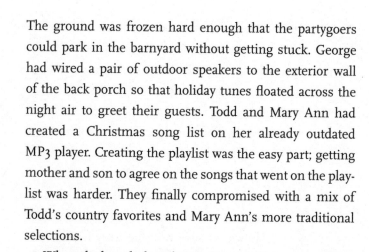

The ground was frozen hard enough that the partygoers could park in the barnyard without getting stuck. George had wired a pair of outdoor speakers to the exterior wall of the back porch so that holiday tunes floated across the night air to greet their guests. Todd and Mary Ann had created a Christmas song list on her already outdated MP3 player. Creating the playlist was the easy part; getting mother and son to agree on the songs that went on the playlist was harder. They finally compromised with a mix of Todd's country favorites and Mary Ann's more traditional selections.

When she heard a knock, Mary Ann yelled out to George and Todd. "They're here!"

Still wearing her apron, Mary Ann opened the back door and greeted the first guests. Only city people ever came to the front door. It was Principal Wallace and his wife.

"Merry Christmas! Thanks for coming."

Mr. Wallace, nearly sixty, sighed happily. "We wouldn't miss it. Been coming out here since I was a little boy."

Because the kitchen would soon be jammed with visitors, Mary Ann ushered her guests toward the living room. "By the way, thanks again so much for lending me those volunteers. The McCray shelter is up and running."

"I'd like a tour of our students' handiwork after I've had one of these little fancy sandwiches."

"I'm sure Todd would love to lead a tour. But I'll warn you, we still have nine dogs left, and Todd's not shy about filling out adoption papers!"

By six-thirty the house was beginning to fill. With minimal coaxing, and recognizing that her guests expected a music teacher to do such things, Mary Ann sat down at the piano and started leafing through her Christmas songbook. She was willing to play, but only if others gathered around and sang with her.

After leading her guests through a few Christmas standards, she looked out the window from her piano bench. "Laura and her parents are here," she called. "Now we have professional singers on board!"

Todd's eyes suddenly lit up when he heard Laura's name. He went to the window. Right behind the Jordan car he noticed the unmistakable old blue Chrysler Imperial. "Doc Pelot is here, too," he added.

As they got out of their cars, the vet spoke to Laura's father. Laura, her mother, and Doc Pelot came into the kitchen where George and Todd were, but John Jordan lingered outside.

"Merry Christmas, George!" the vet said. "I told John to park right in your yard, close to the house. I hope you don't mind. It'll make it easier for him to unload his cargo. Go on out there now. He'll need your help."

"His cargo? My help?" George didn't know what to make of the strange comments and looked to Todd for a clue, but Todd was busy escorting Laura and her mom into the living room. Shrugging, George did as Doc directed. Minutes later he and John Jordan returned with a large, but thin, rectangular object hidden beneath a green blanket.

George looked at Doc Pelot as they entered the house through the kitchen. "Thanks, Doc, but I'm not sure we have space for another Rembrandt."

Doc Pelot motioned toward one of the back bedrooms, where guests had been depositing their hats and coats, and said, "Just put it in there for now."

After George set it down, he returned to the kitchen and grinned at Doc Pelot. "Anything else you have up your sleeve for me this evening?"

"Yes, there is an old man in a wheelchair who just pulled up and he might need your help to get inside."

Before George could inquire about the name of the mystery guest, Dr. Wilson, the young staff physician at the Wellness Center, approached the back door pushing a wheelchair.

George was shocked but pleased, quickly helping Dr. Wilson get the chair over the threshold of the back door and fussing over his surprise guest. Doc Pelot looked down at his friend in the chair. "Merry Christmas, Hank."

"Let's get this party started," Hank said.

George pushed Hank's wheelchair up to the piano. Mary Ann could hardly believe her eyes and stopped playing, rising to give her old sick friend a hug.

Earlier, Doc Pelot and Hank had had to promise Dr. Wilson that it would be a short outing for his patient, so now they needed to work quickly. The vet went over and stood beside Hank and cleared his throat. "Could I please have everyone's attention for a moment? Hank and I, the designated old geezers of Crossing Trails, have hijacked this Christmas party to make an announcement."

A blanket covered Hank Fisher's legs and he looked truly old, but there was still fiery excitement in his eyes. "I've not missed a single McCray holiday party since George's grandparents held the very first one," he said. "I didn't want to ruin my perfect attendance record."

One guest started clapping, and soon there was a round of applause for their plucky elder. They knew the last year had been rough. Hank held his hand up. With use, his voice gained in strength. "Thank you, but there is another reason I'm here, and I want to get to it before Doctor Wilson revokes my hall pass."

Hank surveyed the room to make sure that everything

and everyone had taken their assigned spot. He looked up at his friend and said, "This old man standing next to me . . ."

Doc Pelot tapped the floor with his cane and picked up a foot and set it back down again to let it be known that he was still on his own two feet. The vet gave Todd a wink.

Hank continued, "Anyway, us old codgers decided something a few days back, and we want to share it with you tonight. We thought this was a fitting time and place."

The room suddenly fell very quiet as everyone realized that the joking was over. All eyes were on Hank. "Susan, would you come over here, please? Susan, as most of you know, is my attorney."

Susan Reeves moved beside his wheelchair. "I asked Susan to come with me tonight for a very special reason. Susan has set up a little charitable company—she calls it a not-for-profit foundation—and it's meant to help us deal with a serious problem here in Crossing Trails. Hank and I decided that we're too old to have anything named after us, so, Doc, why don't you share what we decided to call it?"

Doc Pelot pointed to his young friend across the room. "We have decided to call our little enterprise the Todd McCray Foundation in honor of that good-looking feller in the red tennis shoes leaning against the wall with that black hound of his. All of you know that Todd has saved and enriched the lives of hundreds, maybe even thousands, of animals in this county. And because of that he has improved the lives of a whole lot of humans, too. That's why we'd like to name this endeavor after him. Susan, can you also explain what this foundation will do?"

Susan Reeves stepped in front of her two elderly clients. "Doc Pelot has donated the five acres where his old vet clinic sits out by the highway. Hank Fisher has donated the first forty thousand dollars toward the construction of a brand-new animal shelter to be owned and operated by the foundation. We're going to need to raise more, but that's an excellent start."

"There are a few more pieces you need to know about," Hank said.

"We need two hundred thousand dollars, so we've got a ways to go. I know it's a lot for this community to raise, and it'll take some time. That said, we've raised more money for other things in the past, and I think we can do it again."

There were excited whispers and more applause from the small gathering.

It suddenly got quiet, and Todd realized that many guests were looking his way. He wasn't exactly sure what all of this meant, but he knew that some very special gifts had just been given, and that finally there was good news for the shelter. He looked out across the room at the many people he had come to know and love. Like his father taught him, he kept it simple. "Thank you very much."

George and Mary Ann stepped beside him and each put an arm around the young man they loved so much. Mary Ann leaned over and kissed Todd on the cheek. Hayley, Laura, and Gracie worked their way to the front of the room and stood next to Doc Pelot. Todd bent down and accepted a canine kiss of gratitude from Gracie.

With tears in her eyes, Hayley said, "Todd, we're all so proud of you."

Doc Pelot continued, "Like I said, I'm donating the ground, and, as Laura Jordan and Hank have discussed, we always felt like the shelter should have some kind of a monument or sign in front of it that will speak to our mission. Laura talked her father into helping us out."

It was Laura's turn. With her left hand resting on Hank's shoulder and her right clasping the support bar on Gracie's vest, she spoke to the guests. "My dad spent all day yesterday in his woodworking shop. My family would like to donate a sign for our new shelter. It could be located out in the yard of Doc's old vet clinic, right where you turn off the old highway, so people could see it."

Laura's father and George moved from the back of the room carrying the rectangular object still hidden beneath the big green blanket. A space was cleared so they could move close to Hank. Laura took the edge of the blanket in her hand and then offered it to Gracie. "Gracie! Tug!" she commanded. The dog gave the blanket a big yank. Everyone gasped upon seeing the carefully crafted and painted sign. It read:

> *The greatness of a nation and its moral progress*
> *can be judged by the way its animals are treated.*
> —Mohandas Gandhi

Just to the right of Gandhi's words was a drawing of a thermometer marked at ten-thousand-dollar increments. At the top the sign read TWO HUNDRED THOUSAND DOLLARS—OUR GOAL. The thermometer was filled in with red up to the "$40,000" mark.

When Laura started to choke up, her father finished for her. "It's not too fancy, but it says all we need it to say."

Doc Pelot made his pitch. He pointed to the red area on the sign. "As you can see, Hank has seeded the pot with forty thousand dollars." After another brief round of applause, the old vet continued, "It's a very generous start, but I want to encourage each of you to dig into your checkbooks and make a contribution when you can. Susan has agreed to act as our treasurer, so she can accept funds."

George took Mary Ann's hand and addressed the small crowd. "This is a wonderful surprise for our family. Whether or not Crossing Trails has an animal shelter may not seem that important to the bigger world out there, but to our community, and especially to Todd McCray, it is very important." Then he cracked a broad grin. "In the meantime, if anyone is in dire need of a dog, I'll get my coat on and show you what we've got out in the barn."

CHAPTER 18

TWO DAYS later, on the morning of Christmas Eve, the McCray children and grandchildren started to arrive for the family's own holiday event. The level of excitement slowly built as the day progressed. By two in the afternoon, Mary Ann wondered if the walls of their old farmhouse could contain so much energy.

"George, why don't you take the kids outside to play until dinner is ready? I bet they would enjoy seeing what you're keeping in the barn," Mary Ann suggested loudly. Then she lowered her voice and said to her husband, "I can't hear myself think!" As much as the senior McCrays adored their seven grandchildren, and even though they had raised five children of their own, they never failed to be astounded at the noise level of the next generation.

"Great idea." George put on his hat and coat and called

into the living room, "I'm going outside to play. Anyone want to come with me?"

The grandchildren all began to scream excitedly and stampeded into the kitchen. "Yeah! We want to go."

George pointed to the pile of coats, mittens, and scarves by the back door. "Put on your gear and I'll meet you out by the barn."

George and Christmas were both moving a little more slowly after a rambunctious morning with the kids. As George opened the old barn door and looked inside, he let out a very long breath as if to summon up more energy. He motioned to the children spilling out the back door of the house. "Come over here. I want to show you something."

With the children behind him, George stepped into the barn. "We're keeping some extra dogs here now, just until we can find them homes." He showed each of the shelter dogs to the grandchildren. As he was conducting the tour, Todd passed through the barn door, ready to help. He had spent most of the day with Laura and had just arrived for the Christmas Eve meal.

For the McCray grandchildren, their uncle Todd was almost as interesting as the shelter dogs. They gathered around him, clamoring for hugs, and yelling, "Me! Me next!" He tickled, spun, and wrestled them to the ground. When they got back to the business of the barn tour, Todd took each dog out and provided a more private greeting.

With her usual impeccable timing, George and Mary

Ann's only daughter, Hannah, was the next one through the barn door. She had driven down from a suburb of Kansas City. She too was greeted by an excited throng screaming and yelling, "Aunt Hannah!"

Once the grandchildren had gotten their hugs, they dispersed to play in the barn. George put one arm around Hannah and the other around Todd as they stood by the cages. Hannah had heard some of the details by phone from Mary Ann, but she was excited to get the scoop directly from Todd.

"I can't believe they're going to name the shelter foundation after my baby brother!" She squeezed him. "I'm so proud of you. I bet Laura is proud, too."

Todd beamed. "She's proud."

"I hear the dairy offered you a spot. What are you going to do now that the shelter will reopen someday?"

Todd set his jaw in an expression that made George suspect that Todd was not ready to address his sister's question. The tension in Todd's jaw relaxed and he said, "I don't know."

George looked at Todd, somewhat surprised, and asked the next logical question. "If you don't work at the dairy, what are you going to do?" George looked at the dwindling population of dogs. "Is the city going to continue to pay you to help operate the temporary shelter?"

Todd shook his head. "No. The mayor told Hayley that I should not count on that. They may be able to keep Hayley part-time for a little while longer to help you. That's all the money they have for now."

George tried to give Todd a little nudge. "So, Todd, why not take the dairy job until we get the shelter up and going again? It could easily take a year or two to raise that much money and construct a building. Maybe that would work out great. Just something for now?"

Todd looked away from his father and said, "Laura and I have to decide."

George looked at his son curiously. Hannah took her father by the elbow, led him further down the aisle, and said, "He'll work it out." She reached down and lifted the latch to one of the cages. A little black terrier burst out of the cage. Hannah had to move quickly to grab him. "He's so cute, Todd. What's his name?"

"That's Ranger."

"Tell me about him!" Hannah demanded.

"He's about two years old. He's been neutered. He has a lot of energy." He remembered a phrase that someone had used to describe dogs like Ranger and continued, "He's strong-willed, but he's not very good at caroling."

"Caroling?"

George interrupted, "Don't ask."

Hannah held the little furry dog close to her. "He's adorable."

"We can make you a deal!" George offered.

Todd took Ranger from Hannah and gave him a hug. "It takes him about an hour to settle down, but then he's great!"

Mary Ann pushed open the barn door. Hannah's face

lit up with joy. She ran over to her mother and gave her a big hug.

Hannah's enthusiasm for life was written all over her face, and Mary Ann's face reflected it right back. She looked over her daughter's shoulders at her husband, youngest son, and grandchildren. "Dinner is about ready. Why don't you all come up to the house?" Mary Ann grabbed a couple of the older children and turned them toward the barn door. Every bit the schoolteacher, she had this routine down pat. "Run up to the house and leave your shoes on the back porch—hats, coats, and gloves in Todd's old room."

She looked back at Todd, who was putting the terrier back in his space. Mary Ann was having a hard time keeping track of five children, their spouses, and the seven grandchildren. Following the dog inventory was too much for her. "Remind me, Todd, is that Ranger?"

"Sure is, Mom."

"Well, I've got good news for him. I just got a phone call from Peggy Hopkins. Ranger has a new home." Todd looked surprised, so Mary Ann filled in the missing pieces for him. "I guess Frank Hopkins has been talking about him nonstop since Ranger burst into his house while the rest of you were caroling. Says he likes the dog's grit—his 'spunk,' Peggy kept saying. She's coming to pick him up tomorrow morning and give him to Frank for Christmas."

Todd grinned and held Ranger close to him. "You're going to have to learn to get along with that little poodle!"

With the children out in front of them, George and

Hannah followed behind. Mary Ann lingered a minute longer in the barn with her son. She glanced down the row of cages and asked Todd, "How do they like their new home?"

"They'd rather have real homes, but they're okay for now."

"You ready to eat?"

Todd took his mother's hand. "Mom?" He then continued, "Do you mind if I ask Laura and her parents to come over tomorrow morning for Christmas brunch?"

"Of course not, Todd. If they don't have other plans, we'd love for them to join us."

"They don't have other plans, 'cause I already asked them."

Mary Ann shook her head. "Just as I thought. Did you tell them eleven o'clock?"

"I think so."

"Well, make sure! We don't want them to miss the meal." Todd ran off ahead of his mother. She shut the barn door and started on the short walk back to the house for dinner. Unlike the interior of her home, the world outside was remarkably tranquil. She loitered for a few minutes, enjoying some solitude by the corral fence, beside the old weather vane that George and Bo McCray had built so many years before.

Mary Ann felt grateful for her farm, her family, and the time they would have together that evening. She leaned against the fence rail and appreciated the way the horizontal light from the setting sun illuminated the speckled white-and-brown farmscape. Bits of summer grass, showing tints of buckskin and roan, poked stubbornly through the thin patches of snow, unwilling to yield to winter.

She pulled her jacket close around her and watched the sun sink on the horizon. Her horses were grazing in the meadow to the west. Little gray puffs of air came from their nostrils as they picked through the snow. She felt colder air push against her face and could hear the little propellers on the weather vane whirling even faster above her. The sun reflected off the belly of the miniature Cessna as the small plane spun around to a new direction.

CHAPTER 19

IT WAS one of his favorite holiday chores. Early Christmas morning, George snuck down the staircase with a sack of toys and other gifts the adults had put together and wrapped the night before. As the designated Santa Claus, George placed all the gifts under the tree. After he took the obligatory bite out of the sugar cookie politely set out for Santa on the best white china, he left to do Hank's chores in the still early hours before dawn.

When he got back, the children were anxiously waiting for their gifts. George continued in his role as Mr. Claus and distributed the brightly wrapped packages, one at a time, and at a snail's pace. The children yelled, "Grandpa, you're too slow!"

"Don't you want it to last?"

Once the presents were opened, the adults started putting together Christmas brunch, and the house full of family guests took turns in the bathroom lines. George took Todd aside and said, "I almost forgot about this. I thought you might like to have it." George dug into a brown sack and pulled out the old cowbell he had polished up.

Todd looked over the cowbell and seemed strangely glum. "Don't you like it?" George asked.

Todd felt as if the bell symbolized everything he was going to have to leave behind if he moved away, and the thought made him sad. "Yes, Dad. I like it a lot. You're a good gift giver." Todd gave his dad a big hug. "I love you and Mom very much. I have to go now."

Todd went back to Thorne's cabin to change out of his pajamas and get cleaned up for brunch with his family and Laura and her parents. Having invested a small fortune in his interview suit, he had proudly told Laura he was going to wear it again on Christmas Day. After he changed, he put together a bag of gifts and other special items he had assembled for the morning brunch.

Back at his parents' house, Todd sat on the sofa and fidgeted nervously as he waited for Laura and her parents to arrive. In the kitchen, Mary Ann commented that Todd seemed jumpy, but Hannah only grinned. "Come on, Mom, think about it! It makes perfectly good sense to me!" Mary Ann wished she could be as lighthearted about it as

Hannah was, but Mary Ann was thinking about her youngest son, not a kid brother.

When Laura still had not arrived by 11:10, George tapped his watch and teased, "Do you think they forgot?"

Immediately he regretted his gentle joke when he saw that Todd seemed genuinely frightened by the prospect. Just then Hannah saved the day, calling out from the kitchen, "They're here!"

It was now sunny outside and not particularly cold, so Laura took her coat off in the car. Gracie exited first and then backed up to Laura to help her from the backseat. She held the handle on Gracie's vest as the two of them made their way to the back door.

Mr. and Mrs. Jordan would not have chosen to spend Christmas morning with the family of their daughter's best friend, particularly when they had just been out to the McCray farm a few days earlier. That said, they liked Todd and they loved their daughter. Laura didn't ask for much, and this seemed important to her, so they just said, "Of course, we'd love to go."

Not all the McCray grandchildren had met Laura, so some of them were very curious, jockeying for a front-row seat at the dining room window facing west toward the driveway. They were having a hard time taking it all in and started whispering to each other. "Is that her? Is that Todd's friend?" "Maybe she's his girlfriend?" "She's so beautiful!" "Why does the dog help her walk?" "I think she's a princess." "Maybe she's a pixie or a fairy?" "Why does she walk so slowly?" "Shhh! We're not supposed to talk about it. . . ."

When the Jordans were inside, Todd took Laura aside and whispered to her, somewhat boldly, "You look so beautiful in your dress."

Laura held Todd's arm. "Not half as handsome as you." She kissed him gently on the cheek. "Merry Christmas. Thanks for asking us over."

The McCray grandchildren were drawn to Laura and Gracie, crowding around them as if they were the ice-cream truck on a hot August evening. Todd introduced each one to Laura and then helped her take a seat in the living room. As soon as the remaining introductions were completed, the smallest children began crawling up onto the sofa for a closer look at the princess who wore a dark blue dress and her hair tied back with a red bow. Gracie sat patiently beside her. One grandchild had his arms wrapped around the white dog's neck and did not plan to let go anytime soon.

Todd noticed that the fire was fading and asked his eldest brother, Jonathan, "Can you put another log on the fire?"

Jonathan looked at Todd decked out in his new suit. As if that was not enough, now he was worrying about the fireplace ambience. "Are you feeling alright?"

"Kinda," Todd said with a curious little smile. He went back to the sofa to sit with Laura, though he couldn't get too close because of the crowd of nieces and nephews scattered around her.

"Everyone to the table!" Mary Ann called from the kitchen.

The children all clamored for the seat next to Laura and Gracie. Todd took the chair to her left and, after putting the last remaining steaming dishes on the table, Mary Ann evicted a squatter who had claimed the seat at the head of the table, which happened to be on Laura's right. "Honey, please move to another chair," she said to the grandchild. "I need to be close to the kitchen."

Once seated, they all joined hands, and George expressed his gratitude for their coming together on that Christmas morning.

The food was passed and the sound of talking was replaced with the clinking of cutlery and glasses. Apparently everyone was hungry, because for a while there was very little conversation. Todd, never afraid to speak his mind, looked at Laura and all the people he loved most in the world and seized the moment. "I want to say something important."

George looked at Mary Ann curiously. She widened her eyes and shrugged as if to say, Don't ask me.

Todd's eyes were red. He was tearing up. Not big sobs, just moisture forming at the edges of his bloodshot eyes. He had spent the last few nights tossing and turning, thinking about his choices. It was hard for Todd to sort out all the joy he was holding while still feeling the weight of fear and sadness.

He removed and unfolded a sheet of paper from the breast pocket of his suit, an e-mail he had printed out earlier that morning. "I want to read you something." He swallowed hard and began:

> Dear Todd,
>
> I am writing to formally offer you a position as Assistant Dog Trainer at the Heartland School of Dog Training. Please contact me once you've made your decision and we can discuss the remaining details. We would be honored to have you on our team.
>
> Congratulations,
>
> Julie Bradshaw.

Laura leaned closer and took Todd's hand. "It's alright, Todd, just say it."

Todd continued, "I'm going to miss you all very much. I'm going to take the job, and I'll be moving to Washington, Kansas, at the first of the year."

Mary Ann gripped one of the table legs as if that was all that would prevent her from being sucked up into the sky by a cyclone that had descended from a seemingly blue sky. Her heart raced and she could feel herself flushing red. She whispered to herself, "No!"

Just at that moment, as if he could sense that his presence was required, Christmas calmly walked in from the living room and plopped himself down beside Todd. The sight of him prompted Todd to add, "They are going to let me take Christmas with me, so I won't be alone. I'm going to buy a better truck with my savings account money, too, so I can come home some weekends."

George, as blindsided as Mary Ann but a better actor, and wanting to encourage Todd to choose his own path, felt the need to set the mood for an appropriate response. He stood up and walked over to Todd. "Let me be the first to shake your hand." Todd took it. George beamed, though he too, like Todd, was trying to reconcile fear and hope. "We love you very much, Todd, and if this is what you want, then you should do it. Of course, you've got a whole lot of explaining to do before we're letting you out of our sight!"

As the table buzzed with congratulations, laughter, and excitement, Mary Ann leaned over and hugged Laura. She whispered into Laura's ear the words she honestly felt, "I don't want him to go."

Laura hugged her back. "Me either, but this is what's best for him. He is so excited to do this."

Mary Ann knew the little Cessna was changing directions and she needed to either get on board or risk being left behind. "I know. It's just . . . He's still my baby."

CHAPTER 20

AFTER BRUNCH was finished and the crowd around Todd had thinned, Mary Ann and George got him alone—or almost, because Laura refused to leave his side. Although George was less emotional than Mary Ann, he too had a laundry list of questions for his youngest son, wondering how well Todd had thought through all the ramifications of his decision.

Settling into a relatively quiet spot in the living room, he and Mary Ann fired an array of logical considerations at him. Laura sat beside Todd as he calmly assured them that he and Laura and the Heartland School were fully capable of dealing with each of the issues. In fact, they had discussed them at length. The school had student housing for their interns—usually young vet students who came from Kansas State in late May or early June. Until the interns arrived that summer, Todd could live in the student housing for free. That would give him plenty of time to find a place of his own. His pay was generous for an entry-level position. Slowly, Mary Ann relaxed. At the end of the grilling session, there were only a handful of obstacles that still demanded her attention. She knew she could deal with cell phones, address changes, dentists, and doctors later.

Without any warning, without their consent, and without their direction, Todd had gone and grown up on George and Mary Ann. He was his own person now. It was fitting that on Christmas Day they gave him the best and most important gift any parent can give a child. As difficult as it was, they let go. They had to trust that Todd would find solid footing as he stepped out on his own into the world.

After a few hours, Laura's parents announced they were ready to go. They gathered up their things, and while they thanked their hosts, Todd walked Gracie and Laura out to the car. Laura was summoning up her courage, trying to be as brave as Todd. There was something she wanted to do very much. She felt like she was running out of time. It was something that would have been inconceivable to her only a few months earlier, but suddenly she felt she was in the grip of a fierce inevitability. She knew it was now or never.

She leaned against the car and said the words she had rehearsed. Her voice cracked, but still there was no hesitancy or reservation. "Todd, I need to say something." She looked into his clear blue eyes, amazed at how much she cared for him. "I love you very much, and I'm not going anywhere. I'll be here for you."

"I love you too, Laura. You're my best fr—" Todd started to say, but then he changed course. He knew that was wrong. He put it all together—why he felt so good when Laura was with him and so sad when he thought about leaving her. He searched for the right words, because he no longer wondered if he was in love with Laura—he knew it. Still, he could not find the correct way to express how he felt.

Laura decided to make her meaning known in a more dramatic way. She wanted to leave him with no doubt as to where she stood. She wanted to communicate in a way that he would best understand, using her heart and not her words. She reached up and pulled his face down to her level and then she kissed him softly and gently on the mouth. Todd slowly pulled away, surprised. But then, realizing this was the response he had been searching for himself, he returned the favor and put his lips against hers.

From inside the house, looking out the dining room window, an eight-year-old girl announced for all to hear, "Todd kissed the princess!"

CHAPTER 21

TODD AND Christmas returned home to visit every other weekend in January and February. George missed him, but he and Mary Ann could not deny that Todd was thriving. In every phone call home their son was full of excitement, and he could not stop talking about all the things he was learning and experiencing. His voice was filled with purpose; he had the makings of a life of his own.

For his parents, life was lonely without Todd living down the hill, and losing Christmas was also very painful. George felt that the custody arrangement needed discussing again. Todd was narrowing in on a more permanent place of his own and anticipated making a move soon. On a trip back home in February, George asked Todd, "How about letting the old boy stay here with us for a few weeks? I'm really missing him."

Todd understood. "Sure, Dad. I'll bring him back for a

long visit in March. Then when I move into my new apartment in April he can come back home with me."

Laura drove to Washington on most weekends when Todd didn't get back to Crossing Trails, and when they weren't together, their cell phones were well used and they kept each other's e-mail in-boxes full. On a Sunday in April, George, Mary Ann, and Laura helped Todd move out of Thorne's cabin. Laura was going to take a few days off from the Wellness Center and help Todd get situated in Washington. They cleaned and boxed and loaded everything he would need for his new apartment either into the back of Todd's upgraded truck or into the small trailer he had rented.

Slowly, Mary Ann was coming to terms with Todd's new arrangement, but still it was hard. Most evenings she found herself looking down at Thorne's cabin, half expecting to see a light left on. She missed him terribly. For George, it was no better. Spending time with Todd and Christmas had been woven into his daily routine, and their absence was taking a toll on him. He looked lost as he pulled the ball cap off his head and pushed back his graying hair.

Unknowingly, Todd made it worse. He took a box from his father, looked down at Christmas, and said to him, "This one has your things in it. For your new home." The dog's tail wagged excitedly.

Once Todd had his own place, George and Mary Ann warned Todd that they planned to visit frequently. He seemed to like that idea, so they set a date for the first trip two weeks out.

By early afternoon, they were all loaded and ready to leave. George and Mary Ann hugged Todd and Laura and insisted several times, "Call as soon as you reach Washington. Send us pictures of the new place."

Todd fished in one of the boxes and held up the picture of George and Bo McCray. "Dad, I'm going to hang this one first. It's my favorite."

"I'm glad you like it."

"Grandpa Bo reminds me of you."

"Thanks, son."

Todd gave George a big hug and said, "Thanks for letting me ride on your shoulders, too." Then he turned and headed for his truck.

George swallowed hard as he crouched down to hold Christmas close to him. He promised himself that he would not cry when his boy and his dog both left him for good that morning. But what Todd had just said was weakening his resolve.

As he watched Todd walk away, he held on to the dog for another minute. Christmas was thirteen years old, George thought, and there was a chance he would never be back here on the farm again. He held the dog tightly and tried to let his heart express the gratitude he felt for having walked on this planet with such a wonderful dog. Christmas sensed the depth of communication that was pouring from George and moved closer to him, nuzzling into his neck.

Mary Ann put her hand on her husband's shoulder. She knew his history. He had lost a few dogs he had loved dearly, and each time it had been hard on him. She knew how much this parting was going to hurt. She also knew that George would gladly make this sacrifice for his youngest son. If Todd needed the support that Christmas gave him, then he would get it.

Finally, George stood up and said, "Go on, Christmas, you guys better hit the road."

Laura and Gracie were already loaded and waiting patiently for the last of the good-byes.

George kicked unhappily at the gravel in the driveway. He could hear the little propellers on the weather vane spinning. Todd loaded Christmas into the truck cab with him and started to pull out of the driveway. When he was parallel with his parents, he stopped and rolled down the window. "Bye, Mom. Bye, Dad. I love you."

He then motioned to Laura that he was ready to go. She took off as the lead car. Todd followed her down to the end of the driveway, pulling his small rented trailer behind him.

Mary Ann squeezed George's hand as they watched the truck come to a stop. The right turn signal began to blink. There was a long pause, and George assumed that Todd was waiting for a car to pass.

After a few more minutes, still with no change, George

and Mary Ann started to walk down the driveway together. "Now what's wrong?" George asked.

Suddenly, the truck door opened and Todd got out. He was carrying the box of items that had been set aside for the old Lab. Christmas jumped out, following behind Todd as he rejoined his parents.

George looked up at his son as if to say, What's up?

Todd waited for the dog to join them. He reached down and cupped his hand under the dog's jaw, drawing his cool black nose right up to his ear. Todd smiled knowingly and nodded his head in assent. He looked up at his father and said, "You would never believe what Christmas just told me."

True to form, George responded, "And what did Christmas say, Todd?"

The young man crouched down and pretended to receive another canine communiqué. "Are you sure, Christmas?" he asked. "Are you sure that this is what you want? Okay, I'll tell them."

Standing, Todd looked directly into his father's eyes. "Christmas says that this is his home. This is where he belongs." Todd handed the box of Christmas's things to his father. As George reached out to take it, his moist eyes glistened in the sun, and he gave a nod that was so slight it was almost imperceptible. Seeing it, Todd knew that he and Christmas had done the right thing.

Todd looked at his parents, shrugged his shoulders quizzically, and said, "Dogs are like people. They change their minds sometimes." He turned and walked back to his truck, shut the door, and pulled out of the driveway, heading east.

George set the box down and held onto his dog until the sight and sound of the vehicle had faded entirely. He didn't want to let go, but finally he stood and said, "I guess we're both home now."

The dog named Christmas walked back up the driveway toward the McCray farmhouse that afternoon with a slower gait, but with the same confidence that always made him such a special dog.

Acknowledgments

I would like to thank some people that have been particularly good and kind to me.

Gary Jansen and Becky Cabaza have been great editorial partners. They have helped me improve immeasurably as a writer. An editor's job is complex, but at least in part it is surely to bring out the best in a writer and to guide him away from anything that is not honest or true. Thank you to you both. I hope our partnership continues for many more years to come.

I spent a lovely day in Washington, Kansas, last year visiting KSDS, a wonderful organization that provides highly trained canine assistance for people with disabilities. I can't say enough about the magic that goes on behind their walls. Visit their webpage at ksds.org, and see a bit of that magic for yourself. Like Todd, I was simply amazed at what they can do with service and guide dogs. Thank you to Deb Tegethoff and to Larry Stigge for taking the time to show me around KSDS and introduce me to some incredible dogs, and for reading passages from the manuscript to make sure I had the dog-training scenes right. Please keep up the good work.

After my first book, *A Dog Named Christmas*, was published, *Hallmark Hall of Fame* made a film version of the story. As part of that collaboration, I came to know some talented and generous people at Hallmark, and my ongoing friendships have meant a lot to me. In particular, thanks to Ellen Nesselrode and Jan Parkinson for their support of my work.

Also as part of that movie project, I came to better know another wonderful organization, Petfinder.com. Petfinder provides an extraordinarily valuable service by using photos on the Internet to help match shelter pets with potentially adoptive families. With the help of Hallmark and Random House, I worked with Petfinder to start a holiday fostering program a few years back. We called it "Foster a Lonely Pet for the Holiday," and it has improved the lives of thousands of pets. Working with Petfinder has been an honor. Thanks especially to Emily Fromm, Kim Saunders, and Jane Harrell. What you do every day to put an end to the suffering of innocent animals deserves our highest praise. Thanks for letting me help with my small part.

My law office is often a busy place, and the people there work hard every day. To Joan Slevin and Martha Huggins, thank you for the hours you spent proofreading umpteen versions of my manuscripts. It's bad enough having to fix my mistakes all day long; you shouldn't have been charged with a night shift of the same duties.

To my parents, Rod and Darlene Kincaid, and to that group of friends that were kind enough to read my manuscript and, like your mothers taught you, either said something nice or said nothing at all—good job. To my wife, Michale Ann, and my children, your contributions to my life are beyond words. Rudy, thanks for the long runs and your constant companionship. Together we get a lot of work done.

Whether you are reading this book at Christmas or at some other time, I hope the story entertained you. More important, I hope this little book encouraged you to see the potential in all of us, dogs and humans—notwithstanding our imperfections, real or perceived—to make a difference. Thank you to Todd, Mary Ann, George, and the fictional town of Crossing Trails for being the voice that helped me see that it is our task to leave the world, or at least our corner of it, a little better place than we found it.

Greg Kincaid
Olathe, Kansas
August 2012

Greg Kincaid, above, is hitching a ride
on his grandfather's shoulders, circa 1959.
Greg and his family have lived on the same Kansas farm
for six generations.